SADIE

A PALMER SISTERS NOVEL 3

KAYT MILLER

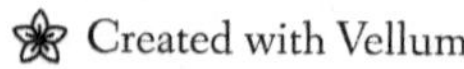 Created with Vellum

To all of my girlfriends who keep me laughing and sane (well, sort of).

&

To my mom, the strongest person I know.

CONTENTS

SQUATTING down behind one of my three display cases, I arrange a new flavor of cupcake front and center. "Mm, yum," I say, inhaling the delicious scent of caramel and pretzel.

"Sadie, are you sure about that one?" asks my trusty sidekick and coworker, Polly. "It sounds a little gross. And aren't those pretzels going to get mushy sitting on top of all that frosting?"

I know, I know. It doesn't sound like it would taste good but trust me, it does. It's the combination of the salty pretzel and the sweet caramel that make the flavors burst in your mouth. "I'm sure. And I brushed a layer of melted sugar on the bottom of the pretzels to prevent the dreaded mushiness." Then I chuckle, because Polly's face tells me everything I need to know. The woman can't hide her feelings no matter how hard she tries. She's a finicky eater. I practically have to beg her to try some of my more, how shall I say... creative cupcake recipes. She's strictly a vanilla kind of girl. That's okay. Vanilla is probably my biggest seller, so I can't slight it. "They're only for garnish anyway but still tasty with the sugar."

"I know I should trust you. You've got a knack for—"

When the bell over the door chimes, I say, "Can you handle that while I go back for another tray?"

Polly whispers just loud enough for me to hear, "Oh *my*. Hubba-hubba." Her voice sounds husky and for my ears only, apparently.

When a deep voice says, "Hello," I look up at Polly. She's boy crazy. Or I guess I should say man crazy, so when she sees one she likes, she gets excited. "Hubba-hubba" is a commonly heard phrase when there's a handsome man in the area.

The woman has no shame when it comes to meeting men. And men make no apologies about the fact their feelings are mutual. I suppose it could be because she's built like a 1950s bombshell with curves and gorgeous platinum blonde hair (because *she's worth it*). That's probably it. When she reaches down to grasp my shoulder, I look up. I want to laugh at my friend's expression, because I've seen it before. She stares down at me with eyes as big and round as saucers. Then she mouths, *Oh. My. God.*

History tells me that I'm going to need to take over, since she'll be drooling all over the cupcakes if I don't. Wiping my hands on my blue-and-white-striped Sadie Cakes Bakery apron, I stand from my squatted position. "Welcome to Sadie Cakes, how can I—" I stop speaking the moment I see him.

Shit.

No looking back.

Shit.

Shit.

Fuck!

"What are you doing here?"

Ignoring my question, he says, "Rachel. You're a hard woman to find."

Nerves flood my body. *That voice.* I'm instantly queasy. Placing my hand over my stomach, I concentrate on my breathing. *Get yourself under control, Sadie.* But I can't help it. There are times I think if I didn't have bad luck, I'd have no freaking luck at all. Doing my best to appear calm and cool, I say, "I didn't realize I was lost."

His chuckle is deep and rich. The memory of the same deep, rich voice whispering in my ear causes my body to vibrate. My hands are shaking. Not from fear. No. I'm not afraid of this man. Well, let me rephrase that. I'm not afraid he'll physically harm me. No, I'm afraid of my reaction to him. In that way, he's dangerous. *So* damn dangerous.

"It's taken me almost two months to find you. If I'd just read this," he holds up some crumpled, white cloth in his hands, "I'd have found you weeks ago."

I watch as he unfurls the cloth. It's a T-shirt. One of *my* T-shirts that reads *Sadie Cakes Bakery.*

"Where did you...?"

"You left it on the floor of your cabin."

"Oh."

Shit.

Taking in a deep breath—*courage, Sadie*—I step around the counter and approach him, holding out my hand. "Thank you for returning it."

He pulls it up above his head and out of my reach, which isn't hard for him to do since he's at least ten inches taller than me. Leaning toward me, he says, "You think I came all this way to give you back your shirt?"

"Yes." *No.* But I'm not about to do anything that will draw out this conversation.

"Think again, beautiful."

Shit.

CHAPTER ONE

TWO MONTHS Earlier

"SADES, you should go. Finish prepping for your trip. We've got this."

"Okay. If you're sure." I *am* pretty damned excited about my vacation. My boyfriend (hopefully soon to be fiancé) and I are finally heading out on our cruise. A cruise we've been planning for months. Well, *I've* been planning. He chose the cruise line, and I did the rest. It's alright; I didn't mind. I've always wanted to try a cruise, and going on one with my man makes me even more excited. The fact that I *know* he's going to propose on said cruise? Priceless.

"We're sure," says my sister Violet and coworker Polly simultaneously.

"Shoo. Go," Polly says, gesturing with sweeping hands like I'm some pesky rodent. "Seriously, go, hon. Go get a mani-pedi or waxed or something."

Waxed? No thanks. Shaving is the way to go, even though

my little sister Keely swears by the waxing shit. I like my skin intact, *thankyouverymuch*.

"Fine. I'm going." Taking off my Sadie Cakes Bakery apron, I hang it on the hook just inside my office. "I love you guys. I'll post stuff on Facebook when I can and text you when I'm in port so you'll know what's happening." Apparently our phones won't work when we're out at sea, so we won't be in contact for most of the voyage. Ooh, *voyage*. That sounds so glam, doesn't it? I look around my office and double check the top of my desk to make sure there aren't any outstanding bakery orders lying about. When I see nothing pressing, I step toward the back entrance of my store. "Good luck. Message me if you need me. I'll do my best to check when I can."

"Go!" shouts Polly again.

"I'm going, *geesh*." Shit, why am I so damn nervous? Sure, it's the first time I've ever gone on vacation and left my business in the hands of my sisters and Polly. I know they've got things under control. It's just... Sadie Cakes is my baby. When I was little, my mom and I would work in the kitchen nearly every Sunday to create something sweet for my dad and sisters. It was also our alone time; my moments with Mom. It was then that we'd talk about having a little bakery of our own someday. Sure, I was young—seven—when she died, but I never let that dream go. Ever. It's why I attended the Art Institute of Phoenix in their Culinary Arts: Baking and Pastry program. Even though Mom taught me a lot, I knew I'd have to learn more before I'd be confident enough to open my own shop.

In the end, going to AIP did more for me than just teach me how to be a better baker; it's also where I met Andrew Winchester III, my boyfriend. He wasn't attending AIP, but he did go to school at nearby Arizona State University. We met at some drunken fraternity party that a friend dragged me to. God, I think I fell for him the moment I saw him. He was so cute, with bright red hair and freckles and light blue eyes. He had, and still has, that boy-next-door thing going on. Not only that, he was kind and sweet that night, introducing me to his fraternity brothers, telling them all that he'd "found *the one*." I sigh at the memory of that night. What girl wouldn't swoon? I couldn't help myself. We've been together ever since, nearly six years. *Six years*. It doesn't seem possible.

Still lost in thoughts of me and Andrew, I slide in behind the wheel of my trusty steed. And by steed, I mean my 2003 Ford Focus LX wagon. Hey! Don't judge. It's thanks to the wagon I'm able to make deliveries. It works great for my needs and business. Honestly, I need a van, but I'll whine about that another day. Turning the key, I do my usual praying to the Ford Focus gods to ensure the thing starts up. I sigh in relief when she —yes, my car is a she, and her name is Fiona—starts up. I can tell she's not pleased at the disruption, but she does it anyway. Like most women.

Pulling out of my spot behind the bakery, I move out into traffic. What there is of it at eleven in the morning. "Okay. So, what else do I need to do?" Nothing, really. I've packed, and my suitcase is already right next to my front door. I've got the plane and cruise tickets for me and Andrew in my purse. I've withdrawn cash and printed off our itinerary as well. I could go transfer some of my currency for the international portions of our trip, but I read we can do that on board the ship. When I can think of nothing else to do, I drive home. As I pull into a spot in my apartment complex, I see Andrew's car. *Yay, he's already here. He must be excited too.*

Andrew and I don't live together, not yet, but he spends some weeknights and most weekends with me. He still lives in Sedona, Arizona, in a guest house on his parents' property, which is about two hours south of Page. My hope is that after we're engaged, he'll decide to move north, but that still needs to be worked out. He wants me to move to Sedona. If I did that, though, what would I do about Sadie Cakes?

For this trip, the original plan was for Andrew to get here by the time I'm usually done at the bakery, around three, so we could drive to the airport in Flagstaff together in the morning. I'm happily surprised to see he's arrived early.

After walking up one flight of stairs, I reach into my purse for my keys but see the door is slightly ajar. It's irritating, but it's not like Andrew to be careless like that. He was probably just distracted. Pushing the door open, I notice my small living room is still dark. *He must be napping.* The poor guy works a ton of hours at his family's extremely successful commercial real-estate development company.

I tread softly into the apartment so as not to wake him, but something isn't right. No, something is definitely wrong. Moving quickly, I walk down the short hallway to my bedroom door. A door that is standing wide open. I turn toward my bed and see him. And *her*. I'm stunned into silence. I have no words. I'm speechless. *Literally* speechless. So, instead of talking or screaming like I should, I watch as my boyfriend of six years sticks his dick into my neighbor. Not only that, I can see from here that his dick isn't wrapped up. He's condomless as he pumps into my "slutty neighbor." His words, not mine.

Ironic, really. I'd always defended her when he'd say things about her, because I thought she was nice, sort of. But Andrew would mutter and even rant about her at times. He'd say how much he hated women with fake tits and how much he loved small, natural breasts like mine. He'd scowl and scoff in disgust, calling her white trash whenever she'd cuss at her two children so loudly that we could hear her through the walls. And according to Andrew, he was sure she was a stripper-slash-prostitute thanks to all the men she had coming and going from her apartment. He also thought that her children were from two different men. It's a likely scenario, since the children look nothing like each other or their mother. But who was I to judge?

I guess he's gotten over his disgust for her. Obviously. God, my heart hurts. I press my palm against my chest but still say nothing. That is until he pulls out of her and moves down so he can lick her pussy. *And that's it.* That's when I lose it.

"You're fucking going down on her?" I screech. I mean, the man would never do that to me. I asked him to do it once, but he scrunched up his stupid, ugly, freckled fucking face and told me how gross that was. Hell, why stop there? I might as well tell you that he never, ever fucked me without a condom. Ever. But for Candy—no lie, her name is Candy—he does both?

"Shit," says the fucking asshole in my bed. "Sadie? It's not what you think."

"Oh yeah? You're *not* fucking the 'slutty' neighbor?" Yes, I use air quotes for emphasis. And for additional emphasis I repeat, "You're not fucking the 'slutty' neighbor in *my. Fucking. Bed?*" I pause to give him a minute. Shit, his face is shiny with her... with *her* all over it. I want to puke. I'm going to puke. I run into my bathroom in time to let my glazed donut go.

When I move to the sink to wash my face, he's there, behind me. "Sade, it's not what you think."

Lies. It's exactly what I think. In six years, the man never did anything with me without a condom. Why is that the thing that's bothering me the most right now? I'm about to say something when she speaks.

"Andy-baby?" she whines in a fake, sugary sweet, Marilyn Monroe-esque voice. "I'm going home. Come over when you're done here."

Baby? She calls him Andy? And baby? How long has this been going on? No! I don't want to know. Once is long enough. Turning to him, I stare. No, I glare. "Move." He's blocking the door. I need for him to move. "Put some fucking clothes on while you're at it."

He backs up so I can exit.

"Sadie, look—"

Holding my hand up to stop him, I realize I haven't yet cried. It's coming, and I don't want him to see it. "Get your clothes and leave, Andrew."

Wow, I'm so proud of myself right now. I know it's shock. Shock coupled with pride, because yeah, I've still got my pride. For the time being anyway.

"Can we just talk about it?"

I whirl around so fast I startle him. "Get the fuck out of my house, *Andy*."

"Fine," he says, releasing a breath. "We can talk on the cruise."

The cruise? He thinks he's still going on the cruise? With me? Well, that's not going to happen. "Sure. We'll talk on the cruise."

Fuck that noise.

"Good. Good." He seems appeased by my cooperation.

But I'm not cooperating. It's a ruse. I just want him gone.

I stand in my tiny kitchen and wait for him to dress and leave. At the door, he turns to me and smiles. A smile I used to love but that now makes me want to knock his fucking too-white teeth out of his face. "I'll pick you up at six so we can ride together."

"Okay," I say quietly. God, I should be an actress. I'm so good at this shit.

The second the door shuts, I race to my one and only front window. I want to see where he goes. If he turns right, he's going to the stairway that leads down to the parking lot. If he turns left, he's going to Candy's place. Why does part of me pray he turns right? Why? I shouldn't care. It's over. It shouldn't matter.

When he turns left, a pain so sharp and jagged hits me in the chest. *He went back to her.* I have to make a beeline for the bathroom again, but I'm able to get myself under control because my stupid, traitorous head thinks: *perhaps he's only saying goodbye to her?*

I step up to my double-hung front window and pull the blind up just far enough for me to watch for him to leave her place. I could lean my ear against our adjoining wall, but I don't want to do it. I wait five minutes. Then ten. Twenty minutes later, he still hasn't left her place. I look down at the parking lot. His car is still there. I suck in a deep breath. *It's over. It's really over.*

I want to cry. I *need* to cry, but I can't seem to conjure up the tears, not yet anyway. Instead, I walk into my kitchen, grab what I need from beneath the sink, and march into my bedroom. Ripping off the sheets from the bed, I roll them into a ball and throw them into a large garbage bag. It sucks, because these were my favorite sheets. Egyptian cotton, a million thread count, and covered in blue flowers and tiny birds. They were a gift last Christmas from the twins, Violet and Keely. Fuck. Oh, hell no. The burning sensation starts behind my eyes and moves to my nose. *That's* what makes me cry? The sheets? But, no. I'm not going to cry. He'll hear me. The walls are thin and I'm an ugly crier.

Tying off the bag, I step to the doorway. Turning back, I contemplate tossing the comforter too, but it's off in the corner. It looks like it wasn't contaminated by the two of them. I may throw it away later. I shut off the bedroom light and walk to the front door. I know everything is off. The oven and stove haven't been used. I already threw away any perishables from my fridge last night. I pat the outside of my purse. I've got the tickets, money, and passport in my purse. As quietly as possible, I pull open the front door and hold it ajar with my foot. I throw my cross-body purse over me, grasp the handle of my suitcase with one hand, and grip the garbage bag with the other as I step out into the Arizona sunshine.

At the bottom of the steps, I throw the sheets in the dumpster and stride quickly to my car. Placing my suitcase in the trunk, I slide into the driver seat and pray to God Fiona starts. She does. Before pulling out of the driveway, I slide my phone out of my back pocket and dial the apartment manager.

"Yo, Sadie. What's up?"

The apartment manager just happens to be Polly's brother and a friend of mine.

"Parker, I need a big favor."

"Yeah?"

"I need for you to change my locks like right now."

"Okaaaay. Why?" He sounds extremely hesitant.

"Because I don't want Andrew to have a key anymore."

"Oh, shit, Sadie. What happened?"

"Long story. Can I tell you later? I've got to get out of here. I don't want him to get into my place."

"Sure thing, doll. I'll take care of it. Will you be back, or do you want me to put the key in your mailbox?"

"Mailbox. I owe you."

"Just make me a dozen of your Blueberry Cheesecake Cupcakes."

"Deal. Thanks, Parker."

"No problem. Sorry about...." He hesitates. "Sorry about whatever happened."

Before shifting the car into reverse, I smile as I give myself an internal pat on the back. I'm proud that I had the wherewithal to call Parker to change my locks. Pulling out of the driveway, I'm tempted to stop just to key the fucker's new Mercedes, but I'd better not. The last thing I need is to get arrested for vandalism. I don't need additional drama. Besides,

Keely would kill me for getting the cops involved with this train wreck. The girl has strong feelings about cops. And they aren't good.

Before I know it, I'm on the highway en route to Flagstaff. If luck is on my side, I'll be able to catch a flight to Phoenix tonight and possibly get to Miami early. Hopefully luck will play nice this time. One thing is certain: I will stick to my mantra. There'll be no looking back. None.

CHAPTER TWO

THERE'S something to be said for luck. This time I had it. *Finally*. Not only was I able to catch a puddle jumper from Flagstaff to Phoenix last night, but the airline let me cash in Andrew's ticket, since I paid extra for insurance, so I could upgrade mine. That's right, bitches. I flew first fucking class from Phoenix to Miami, Florida, and it was heaven. The airline was even able to hook me up with a hotel near the cruise terminal, since I was a day early.

Now that my luggage has been taken by a steward wearing a little red cap and a suit with gold-trimmed epaulettes, I take a moment to look at the ship in front of me. It's mammoth. I knew it would be big, but this is beyond my expectations. I'd bet, if it were on land, it'd span at least five city blocks and rival the tallest skyscraper in Miami. After I'm done marveling at my future home for the next five days, I find myself in a long line waiting to have all my documents checked so I can board the ship called the *Queen Margaret*. Leave it to Andrew to pick a cruise that sounds so pretentious. He told me he'd heard "wonderful things" about the cruise line. According to his sources, the food is delicious, the activities on board are delightful, and the dinners are all black tie. There's even a casino on the ship. Oh, and the events planned onboard are "lovely." His words, not mine. God, the guy was such a tool. What did I ever see in him?

When it's my turn to approach the counter, I hand over all of my documents. The clerk looks to my left and my right. It takes me a second to realize what she's doing. "He's not coming."

"Mr. Winchester? He won't be sailing with us today?"

"No. Uh, he was in an accident. Broke both legs." *I wish.* "His mommy, er, mother is caring for him." I feel a little ashamed, so I add, "The tickets were nonrefundable."

"I understand, Ms. Palmer."

In minutes, I'm given the key to my cabin, a map to the ship, information about all the fancy-ass dinners, the *lovely* events, and the ports of call. "Thanks." I smile brightly at her because, damn it, I'm going to make the most of this trip. I deserve it.

HOLDING MY BREATH, I slide the keycard into the door of my cabin. I don't know why I'm nervous, but I am. It's a good kind of nerves, though. I've been looking forward to this trip for months, and I'll be damned if I let Andrew ruin it. Pushing the door open, I step into the room and gasp.

"It's even better than the pictures," I say out loud. It feels light and airy thanks to the cream-hued walls, cream bedding with gold and black accents, and cream drapes. The curtains are open, allowing the Miami sun to shine through the glass patio door. The room is large, considering cruise ships are notorious for their tiny rooms. Immediately on my left is the bathroom. I step into the small room that holds a toilet, sink with a decent-sized counter, and a shower stall. I half expected the shower to be so small my big butt would be hanging out when I bathed, but I'm pleased to announce that my entire ass will fit. Thank goodness.

Opposite the bathroom are two closets separated by a column of drawers. Plenty of room for everything I brought along. In the main part of the cabin is a king-size bed with a flat-screen television hanging on the opposite wall. It's playing a video about the cruise line on a loop right now. I'm curious what kinds of things they'll play on the television when we're in international waters, but not curious enough to plan on spending my time hiding away. *I will not hide.* Much.

Beyond the bed is a loveseat with a small round table in front of it. On top is a metal ice bucket that appears to be holding champagne. Beside that is a tray with a pretty assortment of sweet and savory things. I assume I'm supposed to nibble on those as I sip champagne on the balcony overlooking the water. Pulling the bottle out of the ice, I ignore the glass and skip the food as I step out onto the balcony. The breeze off the water is cool as it hits my face and an overwhelming smell of salt water and fish hits me. I look to my left and right at metal walls that seclude me from my neighbors. Moving to the balcony railing, I quickly uncork what I now know is Prosecco, not champagne, and bring the bottle to my lips. No need to dirty a glass, am I right? After taking a long drink, I rest the bottle on the railing as I lean over a little bit. No worries, I'm not going to jump.

Ha! Like I'd give that jackass that kind of power over me.

Staring out at the blue water, I take a moment to collect myself. Sadness engulfs me. I'm single now. The man I loved, was going to marry, have babies with, and probably abandon my business for, is a lying, cheating bastard. I thought I knew him. I thought he was my person. But now, all I have left are questions. Like how could I have been so wrong? So naïve? How long has he been sleeping with my neighbor? How many times had he shown up at my place early—to "surprise me"? I close my eyes, searching for the answer. When I realize it's happened numerous times over the past six months, I bend slightly, resting my head on the cool metal railing, and do it. The thing I was trying not to do. I cry. And not over the sheets. I'm still pissed about the sheets, but this is all about the loss. The loss of my relationship. The loss of my best friend, really. *Shit.* That's the part that hurts the most. I considered him my best friend. Well, that's goddamn bullshit, because best friends aren't supposed to fuck other people.

I'm pulled out of my pity party by an announcement coming through a speaker on my balcony.

"Ladies and gentlemen." The man speaking has a sexy British accent. "Welcome aboard the *Queen Margaret*. This is your captain speaking. We're delighted you could join us on the maiden voyage of the newest ship in our line."

"Shit. It's the maiden voyage?" I wipe my cheek to rid it of stupid tears. I recall another ship. Another maiden voyage many years ago. That one didn't end well. I decide to shut up and listen, because the guy's still talking.

"The ship will be departing in one hour. A bon voyage party will begin shortly on the Observation Deck on level seven. Join us for cocktails as we wave au revoir to Miami."

I continue to listen to the captain as he tells us where the lifeboats are located and other safety mumbo-jumbo. I'm checking out the small desk inside my room when I see an envelope addressed to Andrew and me. Tearing it open, I read a note from my cabin steward.

Dear Ms. Palmer and Mr. Winchester,

Welcome aboard. My name is Christoff and I will be caring for you on this voyage. If you have any special needs or questions, please let me know.

Sincerely, Christoff

Beneath the note is a card that states how many onboard credits we have. *I* have. When I booked the trip, I used a third-party company who offered extra onboard credits. Those were in addition to the credits the cruise line offered. According to this card, I have $758.00 to spend while onboard the ship. If Andrew had come, I would have had to split this money with him. But, alas, I'm alone. Which means... I close my eyes to do the math. I can spend over $150.00 per day. On booze. "Hells, yeah!" I don't have to wallow in self-pity because I'm alone on a romantic cruise. Instead, I can get drunk as a skunk every damn day. "Life's lookin' up, Sadie."

CHAPTER THREE

SADIE

"BON VOYAGE, MIAMI," I say, raising my glass while watching the Miami skyline grow smaller and more distant. *No looking back, Sadie.* I sigh at my own mantra. I need to heed those words. I mean, look around. It's beautiful. The sun is shining, the water is churning in the ship's wake. It's blue and cool. The ship is spectacular, the service impeccable—what I've seen of it, anyway. I mean, the minute I stepped out onto the Observation Deck, I was handed a glass of bubbly and had lovely little appetizers presented to me like I was a queen. I could get used to this.

It's then that I decide: there will be no more crying over Andrew. Hell, there will be no more thinking about Andrew. I *need* this vacation, and not only because of what happened back in Page. I need it to recharge. I haven't been on vacation since... since I went to the Grand Canyon with my dad and sisters eight years ago. The Grand Canyon is not even that big a deal where

I'm from. The south rim is only about two hours from home. No, I need this trip. I've always wanted to travel more, but life and lack of funds tend to get in the way. This will be my chance to see places I've only dreamed about. I'll meet new people and do things that I'd never do in my real life. It's my chance to spread my proverbial wings and fly. *No. Looking. Back.*

With my glass of Prosecco raised along with the rest of the passengers' who decided to attend this little going away shindig, I sip as I check out my fellow shipmates. What would you say if I told you I was the youngest person here? I'm not counting the serving staff or the crew. Just guests. I'd estimate the average age of the passengers around me at seventy. I shake my head. *The average age of the passengers on this ship is seventy.* It makes me giggle. I mean, who the hell gave Andrew the great tips on this cruise line? His grandmother? No, both of his grandmothers are gone. I met one of them years ago—his mom's mom, and I hate to say this, but, well, she was a tad unfriendly.

But she had nothing on Andrew's mother, Beryl. Talk about a cold, angry human being. She never smiled unless she was gazing at Andrew. Not going to lie, most of her frostiness was directed at me. When her gaze turned to me, the smile turned upside down in seconds. She has a stick so far up her ass even a surgeon couldn't remove it. The problem is, Andrew can't see it. As far as he's concerned, Beryl Winchester is the bee's knees. I chortle into my glass at that expression. Hell, I bet half the people on board used that term when it was invented. You know, a hundred years ago? I giggle again and squeak out a little snort while I'm at it. Who cares? I don't know a damn soul on this floating hotel.

"What on earth have you found so delightfully amusing, my dear?"

I turn to face a woman who's probably in her seventies, but the work she's had done on her face makes her look early sixties.

Good for her. She's dressed to the nines too. I'd kill for her sundress. I bet it'd cost me a month's profits.

"Oh, nothing. The Prosecco has gone to my head."

"Oh, honey. I wish bubbly drinks still did it for me, but alas," she holds up a short glass with amber liquid clinging to the bottom, "I've had to up my game. Macallan 18."

"Well, here's to upping your game," I say as I hold my glass out.

"Abso-*fucking*-lutely," she replies while tapping our glasses together.

Hearing the elegant woman drop an f-bomb causes me to choke. It was unexpected, that's for sure.

"You okay, hon? Was that too vulgar?"

"Fuck, no." I laugh. "Refreshing. Definitely refreshing."

"I knew I'd like you. What's your name, sweetie?"

"S—" Wait. Do I want to use my real name? This is my chance to be someone else for a week. And I think I need that. "Rachel. Rachel Montgomery." Okay, so using my mom's name is probably a bad idea, but in a small way, it makes me feel like she's here. Clarification. I always feel like my mom is nearby, but by using her name she gets to be a part of my experience, my adventure. And I love her name. Maybe I'll use it again if I ever go on another vacation. Doubtful. It took me three years to save up for this one. It was my gift to the idiot I used to love. Now I get to enjoy it all alone. *Yay.*

Raising her short rocks glass, she says, "To new friends, Rachel Montgomery."

I raise mine. I'm about to toast to my new friend, but I realize I don't know her name. "What's your name?"

"Laura, my dear."

"To new friends, Laura."

"Excellent. Now, let's get shit-faced."

That does it. I spit out the last gulp of Prosecco, luckily avoiding getting any on Laura's beautiful dress. "Oops. Sorry."

"Shit happens."

Okay, I'm glad my mouth is empty. This woman is a stitch. "We need refills. Let me buy you a drink." I need to spend my credits, after all.

"Wonderful."

We mosey up to the bar, each of us grabbing a vacant stool. "What can I get you ladies?" asks a bartender in an accent I can't quite place.

"Laura?" I turn to my new friend. "What'll you have?"

"Well, Rach, I'll have whatever you're having."

I pick up the drink menu and point. "Two champagne mojitos, please." Wow, that sounds yummy. I turn to Laura. "That okay?"

"Delightful, my dear."

The bartender hands me a receipt, and I peek down and see $32.00 listed. Holy shit. I guess $150.00 per day on drinks isn't out of the realm of possibility.

"May I have your card?" asks the bartender.

I hand him the card I received when I checked in and wait as he runs it through his machine. I know tips are included in the price, so I sign the paper and slide the card back into my tiny purse. With fresh drinks, Laura and I move to the railing as the ship begins to move out into the open sea. People are still waving at Miami. I raise my hand and give a tiny wave because, well, because it seems like the thing to do.

"So, spill."

I turn to face Laura. "Hmm?"

"Why is the prettiest girl on this ship all alone?"

Ha! Not even close to the prettiest. The waitresses running around this place are much prettier than me. "Who says I'm alone?"

"I can tell. Call it intuition. Call it a hunch. You're alone."

"Well, what about you?" I know I sound defensive, but I can't help it.

"I've got lots of people with me floating around the ship." She laughs. "Floating." She laughs again.

"I'll tell you what, Laura. I promise you, at some point during this trip, I'll tell you the whole sad fucking story. But, right now, I just want to get drunk and enjoy the party. Okay?"

"Okay." She takes a sip. "Sounds fair, Rachel. Let's get hammered."

CHAPTER FOUR

OH, holy hell. I don't remember the last time I woke up feeling like this. *Dead.* I feel dead. No, let me rephrase that. I *wish* I were dead. I think I drank everything. There's no more booze on this ship for anyone else thanks to the binge-tastic amount of alcohol I consumed last night. Rolling over, I moan because the sun is shining into my room and oh, hell, it hurts. I guess I forgot to shut my curtains last night, so now I'm confronted with the sun, the water, and the glare of said sun reflecting off said water. A double whammy.

"I hate myself."

Covering my face with the blanket, I sigh in relief at the semidarkness created by the white blanket. Closing my eyes, I do my best to concentrate on my breathing, because if I breathe too deeply it'll hurt. If I don't breathe enough, I'll gasp for air and that'll hurt. *What the hell did I do last night?* I remember drinking with Laura. God, she's a blast. I found out she was seventy-seven years young, and the woman can *par-tay*.

All four of my sisters would love her. Hell, my dad would get a kick out of her too. Keely, the youngest, would probably latch on to her with both hands and never let her go. When I picture Keely at seventy-seven, she's Laura's doppelganger in terms of personality and dirty-verbal prowess. I didn't think anyone cussed as much as Keely, but I was mistaken.

Besides drinking on the observation deck, what else did we do? I remember we closed down the bon voyage party, then we moved on to the one and only disco on board. That's what I said, a *disco* was located on one end of the ship. Aft? Bow? Star? Port? Whatever. It was on one of the ends of the ship and hidden away like it was a secret or something. The place was pretty small, but maybe it just seemed small since it was packed full of geriatric partiers who know how to get down and boogie, let me tell you. I wiggle my feet around under the sheets and wince a little. They're sore from dancing. I wore some fairly comfortable wedge sandals, but I danced for *hours*. Correction, I *drank* and danced for hours with my new friends. The part that matters is that I danced like no one was watching and like I didn't give a flying fuck about Andrew.

"Ouch." I wince as I place my palm over my forehead. My head hurts so damn much. "I need coffee. Stat." I should have ordered room service for this morning, but since I didn't find my way back to my room until the wee hours of the morning, that option was out. I don't think I could have handled filling out the order form anyway. Slowly pushing the blankets off, I keep my eyes hooded to prevent the full force of the sun from seeping into my brain. Once I'm uncovered, I look down at my bra-and-panty-clad body.

"Bathroom. Then clothes," I grumble. I step into the bathroom to relieve myself and catch a glimpse in the mirror. I'd like to scream at the sight but that would hurt, and I have self-preservation in mind right now. Back out in the room, I dig through my still-packed suitcase until I find my bathroom supplies. Staring at the rat's nest that I used to call my hair, I gently brush out the knots, then pull my shoulder-length strawberry blonde locks into a messy bun. Next, I use a warm washcloth to wipe away the raccoon eyes caused by my eye makeup and the red residue surrounding my lips from last night's lipstick.

"Hot mess," I mumble.

Back in the main part of my room, I search my suitcase for one of my swimsuits. I brought three in the hopes we'd be spending a lot of time by the pool. I love the water, and it's just what I need today. After coffee. I quickly squeeze my ass into my black-and-white Miracle Swimsuit and search the small desk for my room key card. I spy the ship map and slide everything into the pocket of my sheer cover-up. In search of footwear, I avoid the wedge sandals, opting instead for a cheap pair of flip-flops.

~

WHERE THE HELL AM I? The ship is ginormous, and the map is confusing as hell. Either that, or I'm still drunk. Yeah, I'm going with still drunk. I walk up stairways and down stairways. I walk down long corridors and through openings until I finally stumble upon a dining room. Peeking inside, I notice that people are casually dressed—lucky for me. Walking into the room, I discover that it's a buffet. A very large buffet that must have fifty different stations, each with foods from various countries. There's an English breakfast station. I catch a glimpse of a pastry that appears to be filled with eggs and beans. I swallow hard at the notion of beans for breakfast. That's a *hell no* to the beans.

Another station is filled with bagels, lox, cream cheese, and other toppings. There's a waffle station, and one I'll just call the meat station because every meat you'd ever want for breakfast is there. Once again, I have to swallow down the bile and walk away. The scent of the meat isn't working for me this morning. I scan several more stations when I stumble upon the dessert station.

"This is what I'm talkin' about." It's not just desserts but pastries, donuts, cakes, decadent brownies, cake pops, puddings of every flavor imaginable, pies, and oh, holy cow, the most beautiful mini cupcakes I've ever seen. I reach for my phone that is usually in one pocket or another but realize I must have left it in my cabin. Shoot. I'll remember it tomorrow. There's really no need to carry it around, since I can't use it while we're at sea. But I need food photos, so I'll remember it next time. I stare at the spread in front of me. It's amazing. Picking up a small plate, I select one of everything, hoping they taste as good as they look.

As I search for a vat of coffee, I hear, "Rachel, darling."

I recognize the voice. Turning slowly, I scan the crowd until I see Laura and a young man seated at a fairly large round table in an alcove surrounded by windows. The light is at her back, and it's glaring at me like a sun bitch. Not Laura. The actual sun. I step toward her. "Oh, good morning, Laura."

"Good morning to you too, my dear. Care to join us?"

I look at Laura, then at the man next to her. He smirks. "Well, well, well. If it isn't Dancin' Queen. Nice to see you up and around so early."

Who is this guy and what the hell is he talking about? He's cute if you like guys with a tan that screams, *I've got a lot of free time.* His hair is slicked back with something shiny. He's wearing a pink polo shirt with a logo that tells me his shirt cost more than my lease payment on the bakery. Ignoring his confusing statement, I mutter, "Oh, uh, coffee." I *need* some coffee.

"Sit. I've got a full pot of coffee here." Laura raises her palm to show me she's got a carafe of coffee, plus cream, sugar, and several clean cups.

"Oh, okay, for a minute."

"Rachel, honey? You aren't feeling your best?"

Is she kidding? I arch my brow. It hurts. "No. I'm not feeling my best."

"Have a drink." She holds up a glass with red liquid. There's a celery stalk poking out of the top. Bloody Mary. "Hair of the dog, as they say."

No. No drinks. Pouring myself a cup of coffee, I add cream and open two sugar packets. Stirring it all together, I answer, "Maybe later." Or maybe never again. *Ha! Like that's going to happen. I've still got credits. Or, I think I do.*

Just as I'm about to sip the nectar of the gods, a man steps up to the table holding two plates. One is filled with the fruit I recognize from one of the healthier food stations, the other with meat. Just meat. Avoiding making eye contact with the contents, I look up at a man who looks very familiar. Okay, to be honest, whoever he is, he's not the kind of man you forget about, ever.

"Here's your pound of flesh, literally, Laura," deadpans the man as he places the plate of meat in front of her.

Laura chuckles. "Oh, Charles, you are so amusing."

He turns to me. "Rachel? How are you this morning?"

How does this man, this gorgeous man, know my name? My face must give away my surprise.

"You remember Charles, don't you, Rach? And Cortland?"

I look over at the overly tanned guy named Cortland. He looks like a Cortland with his perfectly styled brown hair in that intentionally tousled look and with just the right amount of five o' clock shadow covering his chin.

"I'm sure she doesn't remember much of anything, Laura." Cortland smirks and then winks at me.

Pompous.

"I enjoyed watching you dance last night," he says.

Not knowing what the hell he's talking about, I decided to just ignore him. I blink at Laura and then up at *him*. Charles. He's beautiful. Just looking at him makes my cold, dead heart jump to life again. Yes, men can be beautiful, and this guy definitely falls into that category with his dark hair and eyes. He's got the jawline of a GQ cover model. Hell, all of his looks are like a GQ model. There's even a smattering of a beard on that angular jaw. His face is handsome, only made sexier by that mouth. Holy shit, he's got a pretty mouth.

"Uh...." I'm speechless.

"Laura, I'm sure she doesn't remember me. She was quite intoxicated last night."

Quite intoxicated? I roll my eyes. Such a pretentious thing to say.

The other man, Cortland, snorts. "Hammered is more like it. This guy," he points his thumb at Charles, "attempted to corral you on the dance floor, but you, pretty thoroughbred, wouldn't hear of it." He chuckles to himself.

What the hell is he talking about?

I look back over at Charles just as he raises his hand for me to shake. "Don't listen to him. The common sense gene skipped him."

The common sense gene?

I place my hand in his and ignore the warm, zingy feeling I get from touching him, because the first thing I notice about his hands? They're soft. Like Andrew's. Like a man who hasn't done any real work for his entire privileged life. Laura called him *Charles.* Ugh, such a pretentious name. *Almost as haughty as Andrew Winchester the Turd, er, the Third.*

"Of course I do. How could I forget *you*, Charlie?" I smile broadly. "Simply *awesome* to see you again." *Simply awesome to see you again?* I want to snort and giggle at myself, but I'm pretty sure that'll hurt. Pulling my hand out of his, I move to pick up a cupcake. I pull the wrapper from the bottom and put the entire thing in my mouth. "Mm, God. So *good*," I say with my mouth full of chocolate and salted caramel. I look first at Charlie, who is staring at me. At my mouth, actually. Holding up my plate, I ask (still with my mouth full), "Want thome?"

"No. No, thank you. You, uh, you enjoy those," he says, looking flustered.

"I wiwll."

"My dear," says a smiling Laura, "what are your plans for today?"

Chewing on the cake, I take a big drink of coffee and regret it immediately because I start to choke, then cough, causing small pieces of chocolate cupcake to spray from my mouth onto the table.

"Classy," snickers a smirking Cortland.

Jerk. I return his smirk with a glare of my own. I know this guy. I dated him for six years. *Nice hair.* I don't say it, only think it, but it's enough to make me feel vindicated.

When Charlie stands to... what? Give me the Heimlich? I hold my hand up to stop him. "I'm fine." Looking over at Laura, I point at my swimsuit cover-up and say, "In answer to your question, I'm going to one of the pools in the hopes the sun will suck out the toxins I put into my body last night."

I must have said something hilarious, because Laura throws her head back and laughs. Loudly. "Oh, my goodness. You're delightful."

Delightful? Where's my eff-bombing bestie from last night? How 'bout "you're fucking delightful"?

"Come to our pool, darling. It's much more private."

I'm about to eat a flaky pastry but stop midway to my mouth. "You have your *own* pool?"

"We're up in the Queen's Quarter section of the ship. There's a private pool there." That's Charlie speaking now.

"Oh." *Well la-di-da.* "Right."

"Charles, give her a key to the elevator so she can come and go as she pleases."

"Laura," Charlie grumbles.

Laura says nothing. She merely arches her brow at him. With a sigh, he reaches into the breast pocket of his suit jacket, extracting a key card. (Yes, he's wearing a suit. At breakfast. On a cruise.) The card is sitting between his first and middle fingers. I reach out and take it. "Thanks." I doubt I'll use it, but it was worth taking it just to see Charlie's scowl.

Standing up, Laura places her napkin on the table. "I'll see you in a bit, my dear?"

"Sure. Yeah." *No.* My recovery will take hours, and I need to do it alone.

"Why don't I believe you, my dear?"

Because I'm lying. "I'll see you in a bit, Laura."

"Come along, Cortland, my dear. You can walk me back to my room." She turns back to me. "Ta-ta, Rachel."

"TTFN," I mumble as I empty my coffee cup.

Charlie grumbles in the seat across from me. "TTFN? What is that?"

Now that makes me laugh. This guy is a stuffed shirt. A shirt stuffed with big, hard muscles. I swear I spotted the outline of abs beneath his suit. Ignoring his bluster, I begin to unwrap a vanilla cupcake with a sugared orange wedge, saying, "So, Charlie, it appears as though you, me, and that douchebag that just left," I use my thumb to point in the direction Cortland walked, "are the youngest people on board. The young-uns."

Charlie smiles, then chuckles, and it sounds nice. "I believe you may be correct; however, besides my brother the 'douchebag,' there are a few others with Laura's party."

"Your brother?" I feel a little guilty.

"And you're correct, he can err on the douchebag side of the spectrum." He chuckles, and it sounds warm like honey drizzled on a corn muffin. *Oh, yummy, that sounds good.*

Flustered, I want to change the subject. "How old are you, Charlie?" I ask, not really caring. That much.

"Thirty-two. You?"

"Wow, you're getting up there. I can see why you chose this ship." I giggle. "I'm twenty-seven." Biting into a fluffy cake, I look at Charlie more closely. Yep, he's pretty. Too pretty for me. "So, what are you?"

"What *am* I?" He looks confused. It's sort of adorable. Then there's his voice. Holy moly, his voice. It's deep and rumbly this morning. It makes my lady parts hum. I sort of wish I could remember what happened last night—how he knows me.

"Yeah. My guess? You're either a stockbroker or in real estate. Which is it?"

"Neither." He says the word like some fancy ass: *nīther.* Ugh.

"What do you do, Rachel? Shall I hazard a guess?"

"Sure."

"You're either a kindergarten teacher or a florist."

"Nope." I say the *p* with a pop. "Close though." A florist isn't far off, right?

"Are you a—"

Holding up my hand in the stopping gesture, I say, "I shouldn't have started this little conversation. Let's just let our lives away from here remain a mystery, shall we?"

"A mystery?"

"Yeah. What happens on the *Queen Margaret* and all that—"

"As you wish."

He just quoted one of my favorite movies, *The Princess Bride*, but something tells me he's never seen it. Instead, it's just something he says. Swallowing hard, I realize I've eaten as much as I can. Drinking the last of my coffee, I stand up and place my cloth napkin on the table. "Nice to meet you, er, see you again, Charlie."

"You're leaving?"

"I am. Have a great cruise." Do I mean that? Do I care about Charlie's cruise satisfaction? No. Not so much.

"TTFN," he says in a deep, husky voice.

Okay. That was funny. I laugh as I walk away. Time to let the sun do its work.

CHAPTER FIVE

SADIE

"LAURA REQUESTS your presence in the Queen's Quarter."

I'm startled from my peaceful doze by the deep voice from this morning. Charlie. Holding my hand above my eyes to keep the sun from blinding me, I look up at him. Way up. He's standing at the edge of the pool. The pool I'm floating in like a water lily. Ooh, or a water nymph. I like nymph way better.

"She requests my presence? Is she royalty or something?"

Charlie snorts, and it's kind of cute. "She wishes," he grumbles. "Please? She'll make my life a living hell if you don't allow me to escort you."

There was so much said just then. I look back up at him and notice he's still in his suit. "Do you work for her or something?"

"No. Why do you ask?"

Ignoring his question, I try again. "Are you married to her?"

"No! Jesus," he practically shouts.

"Boy toy?" I want to laugh, but his face is turning red. Bright red.

"Christ." He glowers at me as he runs his hand through his wavy, dark hair. He's got nice hair. "She's my grandmother." Then he visibly shivers.

"But you call her by her first name?"

"She prefers it. She thinks 'grandmother' makes her sound old."

It does make her sound old, and that woman has a young soul. I keep peppering Mr. Snooty Britches with questions. "Don't you ever dress down?"

"Down?"

"Yeah, like shorts and a T-shirt? You look like you're late for a big meeting."

He looks down at his dark gray suit with tiny flecks of something all over it. He shrugs. "I like suits."

"Nobody likes suits," I say, stepping out of the pool. I'm grateful I wore my one-piece Miracle Swimsuit. And it *is* a miracle—all of my jiggly bits are packed tight. My ass is even contained. *He's* lucky I'm wearing it, because I'm not sure I would have gotten out of the pool in front of this guy if I had been in my bikini.

"I *do* like suits."

"Bullshit," I say just loud enough for him to hear.

Standing in front of him now, I look up into his eyes, but they're hidden behind sunglasses.

"If I change into something more casual, would it please you?"

"Please me?" I giggle. "God, you sound like Fitzwilliam Darcy."

"I *am* a single man of good fortune. However, I'm not in want of a wife."

OMG. He just paraphrased the opening line of *Pride and Prejudice.* "Color me impressed. You quoted Jane Austen."

"I'm glad you approve." I watch as one side of his pretty mouth lifts into a small smile.

I look up from his mouth to his sunglasses, wishing I could see his eyes. I can feel them though. They're all over me, and I don't mind at all. Because Miracle Swimsuit.

~

"RACHEL, LOVE. YOU MADE IT."

Against my will, but, "Yes, I made it."

"Where did Charles run off to?"

"To, uh, change clothes, I think."

"Really?" Her face is mix of shock and pleasure. "That boy doesn't know how to relax. I half expected him to tell me he had a meeting or some such today." She chortles.

Me too.

"This is very nice up here." It's similar to the pool I was just floating in; the only difference is the number of people in this one. None. The setup is much the same—bar on the left, lounges on either side of the pool, and small tables with umbrellas and chairs on one end. The Queen's Quarter, however, has an area with an overhang for shade, which is nice for people like me who need SPF 50 to be safe. Even a portion of the pool is shaded. "I think I'll get back in the pool, if you don't mind."

"Of course. I'll join you momentarily, my dear."

Taking my sunscreen, I make my way to the shady side of the pool. Sitting on the edge, I squeeze out a dollop of white cream and rub it on my arms, starting at my shoulders. As I'm about to add more, I hear a deep voice from behind me. "May I help you?"

Help me? I look up and nearly gasp. Charlie is out of his suit and into board shorts and nothing else, and it's not disappointing. The man is built like a brick outhouse. Shit, he's got abs. Six of 'em. I scan down his body to see his long, muscular legs covered in quite a lot of dark hair. "Wow, you really went all out." I nod at his shorts.

"Yes, I decided to don my swim togs."

Okay, that's it. I can't take it anymore. I throw my head back and laugh. And laugh. And laugh some more. "Shit. Charlie," I say between gasps. "Don?" I laugh more. "Swim togs?" Placing my hand over my softish belly, I do my best to gather myself. "Wow, thanks, Charlie. You have no idea how much I needed that."

I look up at him and see a scowl. A sexy-as-hell scowl. "You find my utterances amusing?"

Oh, shit. Here it goes again. *Utterances?* Rolling over onto my side, I do my best not to giggle. That'd be rude.

I look over and see Charlie sitting next to me with his hand extended, face taut with irritation. "Give me the sunscreen."

Without thinking it through, I hand over the tube. I watch as he squirts a dollop on his hands and rubs them together. Warming the lotion up, I assume. "Turn." Wow, he's bossy.

I turn until my back is to him. Looking over my shoulder, I watch as he places first one hand, then the other onto my shoulders. When he starts to move his hands, I have to hold in the moan that I'm desperate to release. It feels so damn good. Not only is he spreading the sun protectant all over my back, he's using his big hands to massage my shoulders, which were tenser than I thought.

"You've got knots. You're supposed to relax. You're on vacation."

I snort. Sure, snorting is not pretty, but it is what it is. "I'm working on it." I let him rub a bit longer. "Besides, you're one to talk, Mr. I Wear Suits on Vacation."

His turn to snort. "I'm working on it too."

When his hand moves lower, to the exposed skin right above my ass, I flinch. "Sorry," he mutters.

"No." I turn around, holding my hand out. "Let me do my legs."

"Sure."

"You can use some if you want?"

"No, thank you. I tan fairly easily."

I bet you do. His skin is olive-esque. Lucky duck.

As I rub lotion on my legs, he slips into the warm water. "I can't remember the last time I was in a pool."

"Aught-nine," cackles Laura as she swims over to us.

I giggle at the same reference I made yesterday.

I guess Charlie isn't laughing. "Very amusing, Laura."

"I do my best. Now, let's flag down one of these waiters and get our drink on."

Charlie rolls his eyes while I chuckle. I move down into the water as the waiter approaches. I order a bottle of water, but Laura insists I add a drink. I'm not sure I'm ready for that hair-of-the-dog thing, but I add a fruity cocktail to my order anyway.

"Make that three bottles of water," says Charlie. "Laura, you need to hydrate."

Scoffing, Laura rolls to her back, floating next to Charlie and me. It's then I notice her swimwear. A bikini, and damn, she looks, in a word, *fabulous.* "You look amazing, Laura."

"Thank you, my dear. I attribute it to good genes and Dr. McMurphy."

"Who?"

"Plastic surgeon," Charlie grumbles. "He's on retainer."

The cackle that erupts from Laura is loud enough to startle a few of the elderly guests in the loungers nearby. We need to be careful; we don't want any heart attacks. Laura pats Charlie's arm. His defined, muscly arm. "Now who's amusing?"

As I'm about to speak, a female voice says from behind us, "Charles? What on *earth* are you doing?"

All three of us turn at the same time. I nearly choke at the sight. It's a woman, like I said, about my age, but she's nothing like me. No, this woman is my complete opposite. She's tall; I'm short. She's thin, almost willowy; I am definitely not, since my body was made by cupcakes. She has dark hair pulled up into a pretty up-do at the nape of her neck. I've got strawberry blonde-ish hair, and two words that have never been uttered about me? Sweeping chignon. Not only that, she's wearing a dress I recall seeing in a fashion mag at my doctor's office. And shoes? Let's put it this way—the bottoms are red. *Nuf said.*

"Are you wearing swim togs?"

I know my eyes expand to round orbs. I can feel it. Peeking over at Charlie, I see he's peeking over at me too, a tiny smile appearing on his lips. "Yes, Victoria. I'm swimming."

"B-b-but why? You know we're lunching at noon."

I rotate in the water until I'm facing Laura. Mouthing, "Lunching?" I start to giggle.

"What do you find so amusing, Miss... Miss...?"

"Rachel," Laura interjects. "Her name is Rachel, and she's my new bestie."

Oh, my God. I love this woman. I start to laugh again, and I can't seem to stop. This is amazing. Usually, the only people who can crack me up like this are my sisters. But it's happened twice in one day thanks to Charlie (at his expense) and Laura. I do finally get myself under control just as another man appears. Cortland. He's still wearing his pink polo shirt and tan shorts.

"Aw, our resident dancing queen, Rachel!" He raises his arms, sweeping them out like a game show host. "Welcome to where the other half lives."

"Cortland!" says an angry Charlie.

"What, big brother? I meant no disrespect. This is literally where the other half of the ship lives."

Squatting down at the edge of the pool, the man extends his hand. I notice a Rolex on his wrist. "My apologies, Rachel. I didn't mean to offend. Let's start over, since you have no recollection of our meeting last night. Cortland. Cortland Ashbury."

What is with this guy? "Did you say Cortland *Assberry?*"

"Ha! I *knew* I liked you. It's Ashbury. A-s-h-b-u-r-y. Five-five-five-three-three-two-nine-eight-oh-one." He winks. "In case you'd like to call."

Am I supposed to remember the number? Because. No.

It's then I feel warm breath hit my right ear. "Stay away from him. He's a rogue." Charlie just whispered in my ear, and I felt it in my nipples.

"Oh, shit." I let the giggle go again. I can't stop laughing at these people. "Rogue?" It's like I'm living in a Regency novel. The only difference is the clothes. "You people...."

"You people?" snaps the leggy brunette. *Victoria?*

"Oh," I stop laughing immediately. "I didn't...."

"Who are *you?*" Victoria has her hands on her hips now, foot tapping.

"I already told you, Vicky. She's my bestie," says Laura just as the waiter delivers our drinks.

"Please do *not* refer to me as Vicky. It's so... so common."

"Wow." Okay. Time for me to go. "Laura, I think I'm...." I start to walk toward the pool steps. "I'll see you later."

"Alright, darling. Oh!" she says, stopping me in my tracks. "Have tea with me this afternoon. I'll save you a seat."

Tea? Oh, that's right. Every afternoon we are at sea, they have high tea, like the English. That was the one thing about this ship that really intrigued me. But, no, not today. I'm suddenly exhausted and in desperate need of some alone time. "Perhaps tomorrow?" I say, giving her a pleading look.

"Of course, my dear. Tomorrow."

"Great. Have a simply wonderful day." *Have a simply wonderful day?* What am I? A frigging Hallmark card? Sometimes, I'm embarrassed to be me.

CHAPTER SIX

"GOOD AFTERNOON, RACHEL."

I turn toward the deep, male voice. "Charlie."

"Is this seat taken?" Charlie's hand is on the back of the one and only vacant seat at my table.

"No. Take a load off," I say, pointing to the empty chair. My goodness, the guy is formal. I wasn't born in a barn, but for some reason, I feel compelled to speak in elementary-level English.

"This is a quaint little bistro," he says stiffly.

"It is," I respond almost as stiffly. That's exactly what this is. A quaint little bistro overlooking the water.

"Are you having lunch?"

"I am." I nod. "I was just about to order." I was enjoying my alone time, but I spent yesterday afternoon and last night alone. I should probably keep the alone time to a minimum because I seem to spend most of it thinking about Andrew. "You're welcome to join me if you'd like."

See? I can be social. I can't help questioning my own motives, though. Why am I inviting him to dine with me? *Oh, I don't know, Sadie, maybe because you're fucking lonely. Or because the only thing you've done since you stepped on this island is mope.* I've got to stop thinking about my ex—wondering if he would like it here. It doesn't matter. What matters is if *I* like it here.

I watch as Charlie pulls the chair out and sits. Then he picks up a menu. "Have you decided what you're going to have?"

I pick up my own menu and see almost everything listed is seafood. I scrunch my nose.

"You don't care for the offerings?"

"About the only seafood I can muster is tuna fish from a can. No worries. I'll just get a salad."

"Well, then, if I could make a recommendation?"

"Sure," I say, placing the menu back on the table. I lift my glass of water and sip as he speaks.

"I'm not much of a seafood fan either, but I find that blackened tuna tastes savory rather than fishy. Why don't I order that, and you can try it? If you like it, you can put some on your salad."

Wow, that's really thoughtful of him. I'm a little speechless. I mean, I know my sisters would give me food off their plates, but I don't remember Andrew ever being so gracious. On the contrary, Andrew didn't like to share.

"Thank you; that's very kind of you."

After we place our orders, Charlie and I sip our water in silence. It's awkward, but it can't be helped, I guess. I'm about to say something when he asks, "How have you found Saint Thomas?"

"Well...." I pause for comedic effect. "I took a left as soon as I got off the ship."

He stares at me for a few seconds, blinking, then he throws his head back and laughs. It's a pretty awesome sound. His laugh is contagious, so I laugh right along with him. We're still laughing when the waiter brings our drinks. I opted for a glass of white wine while Charlie chose a local beer. Not gonna lie, his drink order threw me. I thought for sure he'd order something fancy like Macallan 18.

"In answer to your question, Saint Thomas is beautiful. Better than expected."

"Is this your first visit?"

"Yes. It's the first time for lots of things on this trip. First cruise, first trip where I needed a passport." The part I don't say out loud is it's the first time I've ever gone on a vacation alone.

Sipping his beer, he looks at me over his glass.

"What about you? Have you been here before?"

"This is my third trip to Saint Thomas, and while it's beautiful, I think I prefer Paris."

In a faux stuffy voice, I say, "Indeed. Paris is delightful this time of year."

"Since you just revealed this is your first trip abroad, I'm going to assume that was sarcasm."

"You got me. This is the first time I've ever been out of the country. I take it you've traveled extensively."

"I used to travel a lot with my parents and my grandmother, but honestly this is the first vacation I've been on for quite some time. Work has kept me busy."

"I know about that." But that's as far as I go; I don't want to tell him what I do for a living. I don't want him to know anything about me, because on this trip I'm not Sadie, I'm Rachel. I'm not Andrew's ex-girlfriend, and therefore, I haven't been cheated on by a lying bastard. No, on this trip, I'm single and carefree.

When our lunch is served, Charlie cuts a piece of his blackened tuna, places it on a small plate, and hands it to me. I reach out to take the tuna with my fingers and pop it in my mouth. "Mm, so good," I moan.

I watch as Charlie places the remaining piece of tuna on the plate and slides it toward me.

"No, Charlie, what are you going to eat?"

Without a word, Charlie raises his hand just as the waiter passes and stops in front of our table. "Sir?"

"May I please order more blackened tuna and a second salad?"

"Of course. Right away."

"Charlie. Thank you. That's very kind."

Ignoring my thanks, he asks, "So, what have you seen so far?"

"Seen? Here?" I point down at the table.

"In Saint Thomas. Yes."

"I've just been wandering around. I spent time at the open market looking for trinkets for my sisters. I signed up for one of the excursions, but I decided not to do it at the last minute."

"Sisters? How many siblings do you have?"

"Four." I'm not sure I'm ready to talk about all of this, but my sisters are a safe topic. I can talk about them. "Lainie, Agatha, Violet, and Keely."

"Where do you fit into the lineup?"

I watch as the waiter places a salad and blackened tuna in front of him.

"I'm the middle child."

"Ah. Me too."

"I met Cortland. He's younger, obviously."

Charlie chuckles. "Obviously. My sister, Catherine, is older by just over a year."

"Is she on the cruise?"

"She is. As are my parents."

"Do you do that often?"

"Do what?"

"Take trips together? As a family?"

"We used to vacation together every summer until Catherine went off to college. This is the first in many years."

"And?"

"And? What?" he asks, looking confused.

"Are you enjoying yourself?"

"I am. Now." He smiles at me as he sips his beer.

"Oh." I feel warmth spread over my cheeks. I'm blushing, and it's stupid. *I'm* stupid. I'm sure he's just referring to his time in Saint Thomas and not me. "Did you just compliment me, Charlie Assberry?"

Charlie chuckles. "Ashbury. Charles Finnegan Ashbury. And yes."

Ignoring the affirmative to my question, I focus on his name. "Finnegan?"

I must have looked shocked or surprised, because he stops moving, fork midair. "Yes?"

"I love that name." It's the name I had picked out for my son, if and when I ever had one.

Placing his fork on the edge of his plate, he blinks. Then something beautiful happens. He smiles. And not just any smile. It's sort of shy and sweet, but it's glorious too. His teeth are straight and white but not perfect.

"Thank you, Rachel."

I'm still a little stunned and reeling from his smile, so I do what anyone would do in that instance: I shrug and stuff my face. "Welcome."

"So," he clears his throat. "Which excursion were you going to do today before you changed your mind?"

"The Castaway Shipwreck Snorkel."

"You know, I thought that one sounded rather interesting."

"Well, if you'd seen the line for that thing, you would have opted out too." I chuckle. "Or is it because you don't do excursions?"

"Not since my last cruise." He looks up at the clear blue sky, then back at me. "Ten years ago."

We eat in silence for several minutes. It doesn't bother me. I'm not uncomfortable sitting here not talking to the man across from me, which is something new. I normally hate pregnant pauses.

"What about Barbados? Do you plan on doing an excursion when we reach Bridgetown?"

"Originally, I had one picked out, but now...."

"Now?"

I'm not about to tell him that Andrew wanted to scuba dive there. "I've not made plans yet. What about you?"

"Yes, I do. Would you care to join me? I promise, no lines."

"Oh? You have Barbados connections?" I snicker.

"Something like that." Charlie keeps his eyes on me. Is he waiting for my answer?

"What does this excursion entail? Do I need a swimsuit?"

"Of course. But that's all I'll say. It can be a surprise. Be sure to bring sunscreen and a change of clothes."

"Interesting. Okay. I'd love to. It sounds like an adventure."

CHAPTER SEVEN

SADIE

BACK IN MY CABIN, I set my shopping bags on one side of my bed and throw myself onto the other. "What a day." I'm tired, exhausted really. My nose is sunburned, my feet are sore from walking, but for the first time in days, I feel content.

Closing my eyes, I think about my lunch with Charlie. It was fun. I might even go so far as to call it delightful. I felt at ease with him in a way I haven't felt with another man. Except my dad, of course. I didn't feel like he was judging me. He didn't harp on me when I decided to order dessert. On the contrary, he ordered one as well, letting me sample his choice. His was better. He didn't mock me when a piece of lettuce landed on my top, or tell me to sit up straight, or that I was using the wrong utensil. He said nothing to me about how much, or what, I ate. It was, in a word, refreshing.

For years, I let Andrew nitpick at me. For the life of me, I can't figure out why. I normally don't take shit from anyone. No wonder my sisters didn't like him. They never said it, but I knew. Correction: Keely's mentioned it a few times because she's Keely and she can't help herself. Violet, her twin, would never say a word. Agatha has always been too busy with her work to bother, and Lainie loves me too much to voice her true feelings, but I knew. He wasn't very nice to my sisters either. He was *just* nice enough not to raise my ire.

Which reminds me. I need to reply to my messages before we set sail again. When I woke up this morning, I turned on my phone for the first time since leaving my apartment days ago. I regretted it the second I started hearing the frantic beeps alerting me I had messages. Of course I had messages. I perused the list of texts before I left for shore. There was a multitude from Andrew and an equal number from my sisters and dad. I chose not to read them at that time. I didn't want my day to be ruined. So, here I sit with my phone in hand.

"Time to bite the bullet."

Looking through the list of names on my text icon, I choose Violet's message first.

Violet: Sadie? Where are you? Andrew is here.
Violet: Sadie? I'm worried. He said you just took off.

I look through the list and see Polly's name.

Polly: What'd he do? You'd never take off on him without good reason. Do you want me to kneecap him?

I laugh out loud. I needed that.

I scroll through the messages, reading them as I go. My sisters are worried. They each tell me that Andrew has paid them a visit. When I click on my dad's name, I wince.

Dad: Honey, I'm worried. Call me.

The last thing I want to do is worry my dad. He's worried enough.

Me: Dad, I'm fine. I've been at sea, so I had no reception. Sorry to make you worry. I'll explain everything when I get back. I'm having fun, though.
Dad: Andrew has been here too many times. He's getting on my last nerve. Tell me the truth. What'd he do? Do I need to kill him? Or better yet, do I need Keeton to kill him?

Keeton is my sister Lainie's boyfriend, or I guess I should say fiancé. He's huge and has an alpha overprotective vibe going on, made twice as protective since they found out she was pregnant a few months ago.

Me: Maybe when I get back. I'll let you know.

I finally hesitate when I see Andrew's name. Do I really want to hear what he has to say? No. But I need to read them. The first was sent not long after I left for Flagstaff.

Andrew: Babe? Where'd you go?

Literally hours after I left he wrote:

Andrew: You changed the locks?

What was he doing all that time?

Andrew: What the hell? You left?

I suck in a deep breath before clicking on the others. The next two were sent the next morning.

Andrew: I'm here in Flagstaff. You already left? You used my ticket? That's bullshit. You promised me we'd talk on the cruise.

Promised? I think not.

Andrew: Grow up, Sadie. I told you I'd explain. Jesus. You don't have to be such a bitch about this. It was nothing.

A bitch? Me? I sigh because I'm a lot of things, but a bitch to him? That wasn't one of them. I went out of my way to make sure he was happy; I always did what he asked me to do. The one time I do something out of self-preservation, and I'm the bitch?

I'm tempted to reply, but I don't want to start up with him. No, I need to cut ties. Hell, I don't even want to read the rest of his messages. No doubt they'll be even angrier than these are starting to become. I quickly send a group text to my family. I might as well just tell them.

Me: Hi everyone. Sorry I didn't get your messages until now. I've been at sea. So, let me just tell you what happened. I caught Andrew cheating on me, in my bed, on my bluebird sheets (sorry Vi and Keels, I had to throw them away), with my neighbor, Candy. He told me it was "nothing," but it was not nothing. He wasn't wearing a condom, among other things. I asked him to leave, had Parker change my locks, and I left. I traded in his plane ticket for a first class one for myself and it was awesome.

I know I sound strong, but there's no reason they need to feel sorry for me. I'm feeling sorry enough for myself.

Me: So now I'm in sunny St. Thomas. I had lunch with a hunky guy from the cruise. I love you all. I'm having a good time. I'll deal with my ex when I get home. In the meantime, tell him to fuck off for me, would ya? Xoxo Sadie.

I hit send and wait. It takes mere seconds before the replies start.

Keely: I want to know what "among other things" means. And what hunky guy? He wasn't a cop, right?
Aggie: Hey! There's nothing wrong with cops.
Keely: Says a cop's soon-to-be wife. Besides, Ian's retired, so it doesn't count.
Aggie: Ian says he's going to set you up with a friend of his, Keels.
Keely: A cop? Tell him no. Fucking. Way.

I'm laughing out loud at my sisters' banter. I miss them so damn much. I breathe in and sniffle just a little bit.

Violet: Poor Sadie. I'm so sorry. Candy? Really?

Violet gets us back on track.

Lainie: Dad is going to get Keeton to kill him. I'm okay with that. So is Keeton.

I laugh aloud again.

Agatha: Ian says he knows a guy too.

Ian is Agatha's fiancé. I knew I liked him. I laugh again but feel wetness on my cheeks. Of course I do. My sisters and dad have all rallied around me. I should have called them all right after it happened. Maybe my trip wouldn't be so damn depressing if I had.

Polly: Your ex has been here every single damn day. I almost poisoned his cupcake today. I don't know what he thinks he's doing. He says he's protecting his investment. Whatever that means. Does he expect you to show up tomorrow or something? What a douche.

I feel my face heat at her words. *His* investment, my ass.

"YOO HOO, RACHEL, DEAR."

I hear Laura from somewhere in the dining room. I look quickly to my left, then my right, but I can't locate her. The room is huge with two levels of seating. If I had to guess, I'd say the restaurant seats five hundred people easily. Not only that, it's the most luxurious and formal dining room I've ever seen. The room is decorated in gold and cream hues. There are at least a hundred chandeliers hanging down over the tables that all look as though they're dripping with liquid gold. As part of my packet when boarding the ship, I know I'm scheduled for the second dinner seating at 7:30, and I'm assigned to table 143. I scan the tabletops for numbers and have begun to move toward the back of the room when a warm hand touches my back. My bare back. I feel breath on my ear.

"Queen Laura requests your presence at our table."

Without turning, I reply, "Does she now?"

"She does, and you don't want to keep her highness waiting. She gets rather cantankerous if you displease her," he says with humor in his voice.

"Well, we can't have that." I turn to face Charlie and gasp. He's in a tuxedo. A tuxedo that looks custom made for him. I want to check him out entirely, ask him to turn around so I can check out the rest of him, but I don't. I shouldn't. Why would I care what Charlie looks like in a tuxedo? *Because he's hot, you ninny.*

"You look...." He pauses. "Wow, Rachel." Clearing his throat, he finally finishes up with, "You look lovely."

Lovely? Okay, I'll accept lovely. Personally, I think my dress falls into the sexy category. I'm wearing the one and only black evening gown I brought with me. It's rather plain. There's no bling on it like the ones I'm seeing around the room. The back is open, and the bodice is a halter-style with a plunging neckline that ends at my natural waist. The band around my middle is thick and ruched. From there, the skirt flows down into an A-line style that perfectly disguises my ass and thighs. I'm wearing a new pair of black, strappy sandals, and some chandelier earrings that Keely loaned me with the matching cuff bracelet. Keely called the look "understated and *schmexy*." I tend to agree.

"Take me to your leader," I say with a laugh.

I feel his warm hand on my lower back, and tingles run up my spine to my nape. This man....

"There she is," says Laura, clapping her hands. "Sit, my dear."

Charlie holds out a chair for me next to Laura. After I sit, I watch as he pulls out the chair to my left. Once he's seated, I take the opportunity to look at the other guests at Laura's large, round table that appears to seat at least fifteen. I'd count to be sure, but I'm too nervous.

"Everyone, this is Rachel. Rachel?" Laura pauses. "This is everyone." She giggles. When she stops laughing, she places both hands on the table, one on either side of her place setting. "I'm sorry, darling. Let me start over."

One by one, Laura introduces me to each person at the table, starting with her son, Charles Sr.; his wife, Emily, who—if I could just interject—looks like she wants to murder me, but that's for another day. Next is Cortland, then Victoria from the pool yesterday. I still don't get the link between Victoria and the rest of them, but something tells me she's got plans. Plans that may just include Charlie. Oh, well, not my concern. Next, I look to Victoria's left is the only person smiling at me.

"Gloria, my assistant, is next, then that's Catherine, my dear, Charles's older sister."

"Nice to meet you, Rachel."

Wow, she's beautiful. She looks a lot like Charlie, only the female version.

"You too," I say, smiling back at Catherine.

She's the only one who's spoken to me so far. I think I like her.

"Next to her is her fiancé, Clayton."

"Good evening, Rachel."

I listen as Laura introduces me to four others, cousins or some other relative. The names have started to blur.

"Nice to meet you all," I say quietly. I wait for the peppering of questions to start but they don't. Actually, the only two people who engage with me initially are Laura and Charlie. I guess I'm happy about that. I shouldn't expect any conversation with Emily and Victoria, since they're taking turns glaring at me from across the table. No matter. I'll never see them again after this cruise. Hell, I hope I don't see them again after dinner.

With course after course served, I listen as the family talks about politics, a family reunion coming up in the fall in the Hamptons, as well as other trips the family members are taking this year and yada-yada-yada, more of the same. I sit silently, enjoying each course from the salad to the palate-cleansing sorbet. Each and every plate set in front of me is a work of art. I want to pull my phone out of my purse and take photos, but I don't want to draw attention to myself. Not tonight.

"So, are you going to the disco tonight?"

My attention is drawn to Cortland.

"Like I told you earlier, I'd love to see some of those dance moves again. You have a, shall we say, special way of dancing."

Dance moves? Special way of dancing?

"Knock it off, Cortland."

Uh, what? Why is Charlie defending me? Did I do the Elaine from *Seinfeld* dance or something? I look over at Laura, who won't make eye contact with me, then over to Charlie. "What? What'd I do?" I whisper.

"You were dancing alone." Victoria sneers from across the table. It's the first unattractive thing she's done so far. "It reeked of desperation."

I turn to Charlie. "I was dancing alone?"

He nods, then places his hand on my thigh. I shouldn't like it. I shouldn't want it there. But I do. I want it other places too.

Oh, shit. Way to go, Sadie. Make an ass of yourself on the first night of the cruise.

"You did nothing wrong, my dear." Shockingly, that's Emily. She's spoken. To me.

Cortland chimes in, "We dubbed you dancing queen that first night. Here. Take a look." He fiddles with his phone, then holds it out across the table for me to take. I reach out and grasp it.

"It's a video. Just hit the arrow."

Like I don't know how to do that. With an internal eye roll, I hit play and watch the horrific scene before me. It's all true. I was dancing. Alone. To a song my mom used to play all the time by ABBA. *I love that song.* For some reason, I can't stop watching myself as I spin and twirl on the floor. At one point, I'm pretty sure I spin so hard that I reveal a glimpse of my underwear. As I'm about to stop the damn video, I watch as a suited form approaches me on the dance floor. I recognize the suit. Charlie. It's Charlie joining me. Except he doesn't really join me. He dances, yes, sort of, but it's like he's trying to contain me. Corral me like Cortland mentioned earlier. His hands hover on either side of my waist as I spin and jiggle. Maybe he was trying to prevent me from spinning my way onto my ass, which was a risk because at one point I nearly fell.

I peek over and note that Charlie isn't watching the video with me. Hmm, interesting. When I can no longer hear the music coming from Cortland's phone, I look down and watch as Charlie escorts me off the dance floor, one hand on my back, the other on my shoulder. He's saying something to me, and I'm laughing. Without looking at him, I asked, "Charlie, what did you say to me?"

Finally, he looks down at the phone. He shrugs. Interesting. Charles Ashbury doesn't strike me as a guy who shrugs.

Oh, this should be good. I pause the video.

"Charlie." I look up at him, holding the phone up for him to see. "What did you say to me just then?"

He leans over so he can whisper in my ear. His breath is warm, and it makes my skin tingle. "I said you were the best dancer I'd ever seen."

Okay. That's it. That makes me laugh. Just like that night. I throw my head back and laugh. It's a laugh that comes from deep down inside. From my heart. I think he meant what he said. I really do. It was funny that night when I was three sheets to the wind, and it's funny now because I just saw the train wreck that was my disco dance moves. The man is just.... He's sweet. Uptight. But sweet. Looking back down, I see I've only about thirty seconds left of video, so I hit play again. I watch myself laugh at Charlie's words. Then I watch as I slap his chest like he's the funniest thing ever. Then... then I gaze in horror as I wrap my arm around Charlie's neck and pull his head down to mine.

"Oh, shit," I mutter.

Squeezing my eyes shut for just a second, I look back down at the part in the video where I give Charlie a big, wet, sloppy kiss. On the mouth. And I'm pretty sure there was tongue. The blush that starts at my chest makes it to my cheeks at the speed of light. I'm really hoping no one at the table notices. How did I not know I basically swallowed his face whole? The poor guy. I turn my head just enough to look at Charlie. He's looking elsewhere, but I can tell he's absolutely aware of the content of the video. I know this because I feel that big, warm hand again. Back on my thigh. When he gives it a little squeeze, I want to whimper and invite it to go higher, but that's crazy talk. Instead, the hand returns to its rightful place on his own lap.

I force myself back into the current conversation. Just then, Catherine leans forward to face me. "You were just having a good time at the disco. Don't let my youngest brother fool you; he was strutting around on the other side of the dance floor like a rooster on a hot plate."

The group at the table laughs.

"Okaaaay, if you say so."

I listen as one by one they regale me with stories of Cortland's drunken antics. The focus is no longer on me but on the youngest brother. I feel a warm palm on my knee. When I look to my left, I see Charles leaning closer. "Ignore my brother,

Rachel. He's got a crush on you, and the only way he knows how to woo a woman is to tease her."

"Like in elementary school?"

"Exactly like elementary school."

I don't know how I get the courage to do it, but I whisper back, "How do you woo a woman?"

I can't believe I just asked him that. What is with me? Is it the sea air?

I don't get to hear his response, because someone from across the table asks, "So, Rachel. You're sailing alone?"

Crap. I don't want to talk about it. I look around the table to see who asked the question. Catherine gives me a little wave and a smile.

"Yes. My, er, friend backed out at the last minute."

"That's unfortunate," says Laura beside me. "But you've made lemonade, as they say."

I have. I really have turned a bad situation into one that isn't horrible. I shrug. "I suppose so."

When everyone returns to eating, Laura leans over to me and whispers, "When we have time, I want the real story."

I look into her dark brown eyes. "Alright." Maybe.

After six courses have been served, including an amazing dessert, I place my napkin on my chair. "*Lovely* meeting you all."

I turn to Laura. "Thank you for inviting me to dinner and for your friendship. I appreciate it." I turn to the rest of the table. "Have a wonderful cruise. Good night."

Surprisingly, dinner was fun. Not as fun as dinner with my family but not as bad as I expected. The best part, besides Charlie and Laura? Dessert. After the dessert, I know I can die happy.

CHAPTER EIGHT

"RACHEL. WAIT!"

I'm already out the door of the dining room and in search of the map I stowed in my small clutch. I'm not in the mood to get lost again.

With a sigh, I turn around and see Charlie approaching at a fast clip. "Rachel. Wait, please."

"What is it, Charlie?"

"Let me walk you home."

I giggle. "You know what? I'll let you, because I've gotten lost more times than I can count. If you know your way around the ship, I'll let you walk me, uh, *home*."

He steps closer. Probably too close. Before I know it, his hand is on my bare shoulder. I feel it slide around me until his palm is resting in the center of my upper back, right below the tie of my dress. What is he doing?

"Rachel," he says in a husky voice. I look into his eyes and watch them go from blue to almost black. "You asked me a question back there."

I know the question. I asked him how he wooed a woman. But I don't want to know. It's too soon. Too much. "Charlie, I...."

He steps back suddenly. "No, I'm sorry. I was too forward," he says as he runs his fingers through his hair. "You're just so damn...."

"What?" Bitchy? Ugly? What?

"Enchanting."

Oh, shit. What is up with these people and their fancy words? I can't help it—I laugh. I literally choke on it. "Enchanting?" I giggle some more.

"Why are you laughing?"

I stop laughing the minute I look at his face. He looks defeated. "I'm sorry, Charlie." I step closer. "No one has ever called me that. You just surprised me. Thank you." Rising up onto my tiptoes, I kiss his cheek. God, he smells good. "Let's go. I need my beauty sleep."

"No, you don't," he mumbles as he takes my hand and places it through his arm. Like a gentleman in the olden days. "Let me walk you."

I hand him the map. "I'm level eight, room 8136. Can you get me there?"

"No problem."

We walk in silence as he leads me directly to my room. He didn't even need the stupid map. At my door, I pull my key card out of my bag. "Thank you for walking me."

"What about tomorrow? The excursion?"

Right. The excursion. I shouldn't go. I like this man, and it scares me. "I don't think...."

"Please? I'd like to show you Barbados."

He looks so sincere. It's like he needs me to say yes. Ha, that's a joke.

"Sure. I'd love to."

The smile that appears is almost as good as the one from earlier today. "Great. I'll pick you up at seven thirty."

"Here?" I point at the floor outside my door.

"Yes. I'll knock at seven thirty."

"Okay." I turn toward my door but add, "Goodnight, Charlie."

"Goodnight, Rachel."

~

"SO, TELL ME ABOUT THIS EXCURSION."

Charlie picks me up at my room at precisely 7:30. Once we stepped off the ship, a taxi was waiting to take us to a marina. "My friend owns a boat charter business. He's taking us out to snorkel with green sea turtles."

Oh, holy moly. That sounds amazing. "Serious?" I screech.

With a chuckle, he nods, "Serious. Then he'll take us to another small island for lunch on the beach."

My smile must be crazy big because my face hurts. "That sounds amazing." I wanted to say "fucking amazing," but I'm not sure how Charlie feels about profanity. I know Laura cusses like a sailor, but Charlie doesn't seem like the type.

At the marina, I'm introduced to Stuart, a college friend of Charlie's. "So, this is the lovely Rachel," says Stuart as he kisses my hand. "You're just as gorgeous as Charles described."

"Thanks." Wait! What? Charlie described me as gorgeous?

After donning life vests, we're told to hold tight as Stuart pulls away from the dock. In no time, the boat is flying on top of the water. We ride along in companionable silence until Stu, as he likes to be called, starts to slow down. Once we've stopped, Stuart busies himself up near the front of the boat. I use the time to take in the view. "Wow, Charlie. This is breathtaking."

"It's one of my favorite spots."

"I can see why."

"Alright, folks," says Stuart. "Time to get our snorkel on." He chuckles.

I raise my eyebrow at Charlie, who must find that amusing because he lowers his head. I watch as his body starts to shake. He's laughing. And I like it. "Come on, Rach. Let's get our snorkel on."

Rolling my eyes, I follow him up to the front to listen to Stuart explain snorkeling protocol. Once that's done, I watch Charlie remove his shirt, leaving him in only his swim togs. See what I did there? I said "togs."

I look down at my swim cover-up and have second thoughts. Why the hell did I decide to wear my bikini? I was feeling brave and just a little bit defiant this morning. I had confidence then. Now, not so much. I take in a breath and slowly lift my cover-up over my head. When I hear a whistle, I look at Charlie. He uses his thumb to gesture to Stuart.

"He's a letch," chuckles Charlie. "But I don't blame him. You look amazing, Rachel."

I know I don't look horrible, but amazing? My bikini isn't one of those skimpy ones. The bottoms are high-waisted and the top ruched and a halter style. My stomach is covered, as is most of my ass. The suit is black, of course, with a bold print all over it to help hide my many imperfections. Even Andrew thought it was flattering, so there's that.

With feigned confidence, I say, "Thanks. You do too."

To say the day was perfect is an understatement. Snorkeling with green turtles is something I'll never forget. They're the most gentle and graceful creatures I've ever seen. Violet would have loved them.

Lunch on the beach was delicious. Somehow Charlie arranged a lunch free of seafood. I don't know how he did it, but we had fresh fruit, macaroni pie, and ham cutters, a delicious salt bread filled with cheese and ham and served with a few drops of Bajan Pepper Sauce. For dessert we ate conkies, which are pumpkin, cornmeal, sweet potatoes, and coconut along with local spices all wrapped in banana leaves. Perfect. Everything was perfect, even my companion. Especially my companion. He was sweet and funny. I haven't laughed so much since the last time I was out with my sisters. Who knew this stuffy man could have so many humorous stories to tell?

At my cabin door, Charlie and I said goodnight. We made it back in time to go to dinner, but I chose to stay in, having had the forethought to order room service before I left.

"Thank you for a wonderful day, Charlie."

"You're very welcome, Rachel."

"See you later?"

Charlie seems hesitant. Unsure. I know he won't try to do whatever he was going to do last night. I'm pretty sure I made myself clear. "Of course. Goodnight."

"Night."

I step into my room and let the door shut behind me. No looking back.

SADIE

THE NEXT TWO days of the trip fly by. I spent one day in Saint Maarten shopping and sightseeing, where I bumped into Charlie at a café while he was eating lunch with Victoria and Cortland. He invited me to join them, but I declined, saying I had more shopping to do.

Walking into the dining room, I feel a little sad. It's my last night on the ship. I glimpse Laura and her entire clan at their large table but only wave from my table across the room. I notice a smile from Charlie, but then he turns his attention to Victoria, who is beside him. I'm not sure why, but that bothers me a little.

My table, the one reserved for Andrew and me, is off to the side. I've been seated with a couple from Missoula, Montana, who are on their twenty-fourth cruise. The company isn't bad, and dinner is delicious. I can say, happily, that I took photos of each course. And dessert, a vanilla crème brûlée, is so yummy I decide I need to come up with a cupcake by the same name.

Strange. It's the first time I've thought about the bakery in days. Or my family, for that matter. It's like I'd been immersed in this trip. But now that the bakery comes to mind, I feel a longing I can't describe. I miss it. So much. I miss my sisters, Dad, and Polly too.

After dinner, I make my way out to the observation deck. It's dark, but the moon is full, so that helps illuminate the people enjoying their nightcaps. The bar is still open, so I use what is left of my onboard credits to buy myself a bottle of Prosecco. I've come to love this stuff. Declining a glass, I walk around the side of the ship to one of the lounge chairs. Flopping down onto an empty seat, I open the bottle and start sipping. I'm not sure how long I sit in silence. It feels like hours but only minutes, if that makes any sense. I'm jarred out of my thoughts when a person sits on the lounge chair beside me. I know who it is. Without a word, I hold up the bottle.

He takes it and drinks from it. "Nice night," he says softly.

"Lovely." See? I can speak Charlie Ashbury.

When he hands me back my bottle, I place it to my lips and take a drink, then place it on the deck. Inhaling a breath for courage, I stand up and turn so I'm facing his seat. Holding my hand out, I wait for him to take it. When he does, I say, "Come on, Charlie. Show me what you've got."

We walk hand-in-hand all the way to my room. I unlock my door, step inside holding the door for him. The second the door clicks shut, Charlie takes over. "You want to see what I've got, sweetheart?"

Oh, shit. His voice is deep and growly.

"Yes," I hiss. "Show me."

In seconds, he has my back up against my door. His mouth is on mine in a fierce kiss. His tongue takes control of my mouth, and I like it. So much so, I let him devour me. One of his hands slides beneath the hem of my short cocktail dress while the other reaches back and unzips me. God, his hands. He never stops kissing me as my dress falls to the floor. Stepping back, Charlie stands completely still, staring at me. "Fucking gorgeous, Rachel."

In this moment, I wish he knew my real name. Calling me by my mom's name in a situation like that is weird. Awkward. More than that, I want my name falling from his lips. *Sadie....*

I stand in my little hallway in only panties, since I didn't need a bra with my dress. His breathing starts to sound labored, almost like panting. Mine matches his. I don't ever remember being this turned on in my life. I stand, waiting. When he finally moves, he walks backwards, taking off his jacket first, tossing it into the corner. Next, he removes his cuff links, one at time, and places them on the nightstand beside him. Real honest-to-goodness cuff links. It's the sexiest move of all time. I should know; I've seen my share of porn, since Andrew needs to watch porn to "get in the mood." He moves his hands to the front of his shirt and begins to unbutton. He slowly pulls the shirt out from the waistband of his pants and takes it off, thrown somewhere in the room.

I gaze at him, and my breathing stops as he unbuckles his belt; the clinking sound as it comes undone will forever be etched in my mind. When he unbuttons, then begins to unzip his pants, I lean forward. I want to see him. But just as he's about to undo it all the way, he stops.

"No," I say, sounding disappointed.

His laugh throws me off. *Why is he laughing?* He sits on the corner of my bed. With one hand on each of his knees he says, "Come here."

Oh, man. He's bossy. Never in my wildest fantasies did I think I'd get turned on by bossiness. Surprise! I do. I guess I haven't moved because the next thing out of his mouth is, "Now."

Oh. Holy. Hotness.

I move quickly then, stepping right in front of him. I'm feeling dizzy. I'm not sure if that's from nerves or from excitement.

"You're the most beautiful thing I've ever seen, Rachel," Charlie says in his rich, deep voice.

Why I think it'd be a good idea to snort just then, I don't know. But it's funny. I mean... me? The most gorgeous thing he's ever seen? Highly doubtful.

"You don't believe me?" His hand moves down to cover his zipper. "See what you do to me? I've spent this entire cruise with a hard-on."

I looked down at his pants. He's right. I guess he must like what he sees because I can see how hard he is.

"You have?" I whisper.

Without another word, he reaches out his hands, placing one on each of my wide hips. One of his fingers glides gently across the elastic band of my panties like he just wanted to feel them. That same finger moves down the leg of my panties. It slides beneath the elastic and moves toward my center. Once there, he uses the same finger to pull my undies to the side. Luckily, I lady-scaped earlier in the day. I'm mostly bare down there. I stare down at his hand. Waiting.

"Spread your legs for me, angel."

One at a time, I move my legs apart.

"Good girl."

Oh, crap. Those two words get me. I know I've got to be drenched now.

His finger moves between my folds, back, then forward, each time, circling my clit.

"Play with your breasts for me, Rachel."

I move my hands up to cup myself.

"Pluck your nipples."

"Charlie," I breathe out. His finger is now pressing into me, pumping in and out.

"Do it," he grumbles.

I tug at my nipples just like he said, making my arousal quadruple.

"Do you like that, my darling?" he asks as he watches me touch myself.

My darling? Oh God, that's so damn sweet. "I do."

"Feed one to me now, honey."

Without a thought, I do as he asks.

I lean down until his mouth is a mere half inch from my right nipple. His tongue swipes at the tip, and I moan loudly. I move in closer and widen my legs for him without him asking. "More," I moan.

"You want more, Rachel?"

"Yes. Please?" I whine.

"Since you asked so nicely."

Before I have time to process anything, my panties are gone. I'm being pulled toward the balcony door. When it opens, warm sea air hits my face and naked body. The sensation is erotic.

"Move to the railing. Place your hands on them. Bend at the waist. Stick your ass out," he says in a demanding tone.

So many orders. It's driving me crazy. I can hardly wait. I move to the edge, grip the railing, and bend at the waist.

"Arch your back for me. Show me."

I do it.

"Gorgeous."

I hear the sound of his zipper. Then that clinking sound as his pants and belt hit the ground. I want to turn around. I want to see him, but I stay put. Oh, who am I kidding? I peek, but the only thing I glimpse are his dark boxers.

"Are you on birth control, Rachel?"

"Yes."

"I'm clean. Are you?"

"Yes." Shit, Andrew always wore.... No. Sadie. Don't go there. "Yes."

When his big, warm hands touch my waist, I squeak. They move up and around to my breasts. He squeezes and teases my nipples just like I'd done earlier. "Are you ready for me, Rachel?"

"Yes. Hurry." God, I'm so needy.

"Stop squirming."

I do. I stop squirming, holding my breath. He's at my entrance. I arch my back and move my bottom out toward him.

"Good God, Rachel."

Without warning, he presses all the way into me, and it's almost painful. I wince and squeak because he feels so big inside of me. In no time, the pain is gone. The further he presses inside, the more blissed out I am.

"You okay?"

"Yeah, I— Just don't stop. Whatever you do, don't stop."

"All right, honey, I won't stop. Keep your hands on the railing."

Oh my God. His arms are wrapped around me, holding me close, and my back's against his chest. He's holding me so tight that when he thrusts inside, I barely move. His mouth is against my ear as he whispers filthy things. "You feel so good. Your pussy feels like warm honey. I never want to stop. I knew you'd feel like this, Rachel."

I hold onto the railing so tightly, my knuckles turn white, but I don't care. Sweat drips down my neck onto my breasts. I'm close. Part of me wants to reach down and help myself get there, but I don't need to, because his hand slides down from my breasts to my clit. He pinches it between two fingers, and that's all I need. I explode and yell so loudly I'm sure every passenger on my side of the ship can hear me. But I don't give a fuck. That was the best orgasm I'd ever had. His body tenses up behind me as he pumps into me harder. I swear to God, it feels like I'm going to come again.

"Jesus," he mutters, his breathing labored. "You're going to ruin me."

He's going to ruin me too.

CHAPTER TEN

SADIE
Current day

"THINK AGAIN, BEAUTIFUL."

I must be shaking my head, because the expression on Charlie's face is one of confusion.

"How? W-why are you here?"

God, I can smell his cologne. It's the same as I remember. Musky and expensive. What is it they say about scent? That it's one of the strongest memory triggers? Well, I can vouch for that. Now, I can't stop thinking about him... about that night. I just held out my hand and led him to my bed. When have I ever been that ballsy? Never. That's when. But, for some reason, I decided to take the risk. I knew I'd never see him again. Or so I thought. So, when I said, *"Come on, Charlie. Show me what you've got,"* he took my hand and followed me back to my cabin in silence. I think the silence only added to the anticipation.

The promise of sex. Sex with a stranger, of sorts. Something I'd never done before. I'm a good girl. Or I was before that night.

"You left without saying goodbye."

Uh, what? Lost in my thoughts from that night, I squeeze my legs together in an attempt to hide my arousal. I'm sure I'm flushed, because my face feels hot and a tad clammy. I nod because I'm in a fog. And slightly nauseous. I'm afraid to speak. "How did you find me?"

He holds up the T-shirt. "Google."

Google? *Fuck me.*

"Your name isn't Rachel."

I shake my head. "It's Sadie."

"I know." He gives me a small smile. "Sadie Palmer. It suits you."

I'm starting to gather my wits about me. "You came here to say goodbye?" This makes no sense. "To return my shirt?" I ask, absently pointing at the white cloth in his hand.

It's his turn to shake his head. "I'm keeping the shirt."

"Okay." Looking down at the floor, I watch his feet as he takes one step closer to me. I was several feet away from him, but now the gap is closing. Fast. When I look up, he's inches away. "You left me. Alone in your bed. After the best goddamn night of my life, Sadie."

The best goddamn night of his life? Where do I start with that? First of all, he just cussed. I never expected to hear profanity from his lips.

Correction. I do recall hearing him say things. Naughty things. The man has quite a dirty mouth in the right situation.

And secondly, it was the best night of his life? Who has he been sleeping with? Trolls? Hell, what am I saying? It was the best night of *my* life too. I never knew sex could be like that. Andrew was my one and only. Sex with Charlie was more intimate than anything Andrew and I *ever* did. But I'm not going to ruin this by thinking about that dickhead.

"The best night?"

"Yes."

Charlie and I continue to stare at one another. I'm not sure what to say next. What *is* there to say? Well, I can think of a few things we could talk about, but now isn't the time, and the entrance to my bakery isn't the place.

"Where are you staying?"

"Sedona. Laura has a home there."

Of course he's staying in Sedona. I should introduce him to Andrew; they could be buddies. Hell, they're probably neighbors. "Oh."

"But I've just booked a room at the hotel here in town."

"You have?"

"I have." He nods slowly.

"Why?" I'm serious. Why?

Charlie's right brow arches so high it's almost comical. I wait for a response, but it's not coming yet.

Without another word, I see the white shirt drop to the floor in my peripheral vision, and the next thing I know, I'm wrapped up in his big, warm arms. "Because," he breathes, "I can't seem to get you out of my head, Ra— Sadie. I'm here to figure out why that is."

"Oh."

When his lips meet mine, they're tentative. Not like that last night on the ship. There was nothing tentative about this man back then. When I asked him to show me what he had, he didn't disappoint. At. All.

I'm not sure why, but I let him kiss me. Why not? It's not like anyone else has wanted to kiss me lately. Besides, I happen to enjoy this man's mouth on me. All over me. However, doing it right now, in the middle of my place of business? It's not ideal.

My stomach flops angrily at me. I pull away from him quickly, cover my mouth, and race to the back of the shop to my one and only restroom. I have to move fast before it's too late.

Slapping the door open, I stumble to the toilet, drop to my knees, and "release the Kraken," as Keely would say.

"What the hell just happened, honey?" Polly says from behind me. "Who was that guy?"

"Just... my stomach's upset. Flu. He's—" I vomit again.

"Uh-huh. The flu that you've had every morning for the past month. Perhaps you should go to the doctor? You've either got the world's worst flu bug or a bun in the oven."

I retch again at the words. "Please, Polly. Go away."

"Sure thing. But when you're feeling better, we need to talk."

I hear the door click shut behind me, and for a second, I wish I could get flushed away too. She's right. I need to go to the doctor. But he's going to tell me what I already know—I'm pregnant.

Charles

I WATCH as the buxom blonde steps through two swinging saloon-style doors, entering from the back of the bakery. "Is she okay?"

"Yes." She smiles, then shrugs. "No. It depends."

Okay, that makes no sense.

"Are you from the cruise?" she asks tentatively.

"Yes, I'm Charles, er, Charlie." I wait for her to tell me her name, but she doesn't. "And you are?"

"Polly," she says hastily. "She never mentioned a name."

I watch as the blonde takes a few steps closer. Her voice lowers to a whisper. "If you're here to sleep with her, just leave. She's been through a lot lately." The woman turns her head like she's making sure Sadie isn't coming through the swinging doors. Taking one more step toward me, she adds, "Seriously. If you're here for kicks, you should go. That girl," she points toward the back, "is my best friend and the sweetest, kindest person I know. She hides it behind a thick skin, but it's there."

"I think I know that."

"Are you here just to play, or are you here for a purpose?"

Good question. "I can't answer that. I'm here because I need to be."

The blonde woman nods, all the while staring at my face. Her eyes move down from there to my feet and back up. "She sure can pick 'em," she laughs.

I'm not sure what that means, but I hope it's a good thing.

She raises her hand, holding it out for a shake. I place mine in hers and nearly fall to my knees at the strength of her handshake. As she moves in closer, her whisper becomes ominous. "Charlie? Some friendly advice?"

"All right."

"If you hurt her, I will *end* you."

Why do I get the feeling from this diminutive woman that she could do it? "Understood." Damn, this Polly woman is a pit bull. She and my grandmother would get along famously.

"Is she okay?"

"Just a little morn... nausea. The flu. Yeah, just the flu."

She was about to say morning sickness. *What in the ever-loving hell?* "Is she...?"

Polly looks at me blankly. "Huh?"

She's going to play dumb, but I know a work-around here. "I'm a doctor. Would you mind if I checked on her?"

"A doctor?" she squeaks. "Serious?"

"Serious. Now, can you please take me to her?"

"Sure." She points at the swinging door. "Through there, all the way back."

I move quickly through the door and then through the bakery kitchen, where it looks like a bomb went off. Flour covers a long stainless steel countertop; an enormous mixer is swirling up something white and fluffy, and large containers that hold ingredients are here and there. While it looks like a mess, I think it's supposed to. It's what a busy bakery looks like. And if the scent coming from one of the ovens is any indication, it's a successful bakery. I smile to myself. Of course it's successful. I've no doubt Sadie is the best at what she does.

"Sadie?" I ask, knocking on the small white door. I hear mutterings and something falling to the ground.

"Go away," says the tiny voice from behind the door.

"I'm a doctor. I—"

"You're a doctor?" she says weakly.

"I am. Please. Let me see you, Sadie."

I hear the knob click, hoping it's unlocking. When the door pops open, I push it open slowly. She's on the floor, arm resting on the toilet seat, back against the wall. Her legs are stretched out in front of her. With me in the space with her, there's no room for much else. "Sadie?"

"Yeah?"

I squat down in front of her and place my palm on her forehead. No fever, but she's clammy. I reach down and place my fingers on the pulse on her wrist and count as I look at my watch. "Your pulse is slightly elevated."

"Okay," she practically whispers.

Next, I turn her hand over and pinch a small amount of skin on the top of her hand. I don't like it. "You appear to be dehydrated."

"Is that bad?" She looks concerned.

"It's not good." I look down at her jean-clad legs and see them covered in flour. "Sadie?"

I look into her eyes. We stare in silence for a while.

"Yeah?" Sadie sounds a little stronger.

"Are you pregnant?"

With a sigh, she runs her hands through her hair, pushing it back into place. "Yes, Charlie. I'm pregnant."

"Is it mine?"

"Yep." She ends the word with a popping sound.

Asking as gently as I can: "You said you were on birth control that night?"

She looks into my eyes. Hers start to shimmer. I hope she's not going to cry. I observe her closely. No tears fall, but I get the feeling she stopped them with sheer will. "I was on birth control, but I hadn't gotten my shot before the trip because we...."

"We?"

"Charlie?" she asks weakly.

"Yes?"

"Can we talk about this later?"

Okay then. I nod. "Are you feeling well enough to stand?"

"Yes." I help her up. "Are you able to leave the bakery for a bit?"

She nods.

"Let's get you to a doctor. You don't want to mess around with dehydration when you're pregnant."

"Fine," she says, releasing a breath. She sounds frustrated. Irritated.

I take her hand in mine and lead her through the swinging doors again. A few customers are lined up; Polly is helping them.

"Hey, Polls. I'm going to see the doc. Be back as soon as I can."

"No worries, hon. Violet will be here in a little while. We've got this."

I look at Sadie. "Who's Violet?"

"My sister."

Right. Good. "When we get the all-clear from your doctor, I'd like to sit down and talk about everything."

"Fine."

She doesn't sound happy about it, but that's okay.

CHAPTER TWELVE

SADIE

"YOU'RE PREGNANT."

"I know, Dr. McCormick. I did a pregnancy test a few days ago."

"You're dehydrated."

"Yeah. Just as Charlie predicted," I mumble. "He's a doctor." Apparently.

"May I ask you something?"

I nod.

"Do you plan to keep the baby?"

Oh, wow. That thought never.... I never considered. Luckily, that's still a choice I have, but the answer is, "Yes. I'm keeping my baby."

"Is that your young man out there?"

My young man? I want to giggle at Dr. McCormick's expression. He's old-school, and by that, I mean he's about 110 years old. He's *literally* old school.

"I don't know, Doc. Maybe."

"Is the baby his?"

"It is." And why didn't he say anything when he found out? He was so calm, cool, and collected. You'd think hearing you're about to be a father would have gotten some kind of reaction. Unless... what if he already has a family? No, I would have met them, or at the very least heard about them. Laura would have blabbed about that at some point.

"He's a physician?"

I nod.

"Shall we include him in our discussion about your baby?"

Baby? Holy shit. I've got a baby growing inside me. "I guess we should." I shrug.

I watch as my doctor picks up his phone. I hear him muttering things into the receiver. Minutes later, there's a knock on the door. "Dr. Mac? Dr. Ashbury is here."

Dr. McCormick stands and rounds his desk, meeting Charlie at the door. "Come on in, my boy."

Charlie steps into the room. When his eyes rest on mine, he smiles sweetly. "You okay, Sadie?"

"She will be. Have a seat. Now tell me, what's your specialty?"

Oh, that's a good question. I had no idea he was a doctor. Hell, I don't know anything about him. Except he knocked me up. And he's amazing in the sack.

"Orthopedic surgery, Dr. McCormick."

"Ah, excellent choice."

I look over at Charlie. "What does that mean?"

Charlie takes the chair next to mine. Turning his body to face me, he explains, "I deal with the musculoskeletal system. Specifically, my area relates to sports medicine. I treat athletes who've suffered season-ending and sometimes career-ending injuries."

"Oh." What the hell? "That's cool."

Charlie chuckles, then reaches his hand over to take mine in his. "How is she, Dr. McCormick?"

"Call me Sam, son."

"Sure thing. I'm Charles... Charlie."

Oh, he's adopted my name for him. That's sort of cute.

"She's dehydrated, as you predicted. She believes she's about two months along, so we'll do an ultrasound in a week or two to see how everything's going in there." Dr. McCormick chuckles. "We need to get you on prenatal vitamins and folic acid as well, sweetheart."

I nod. God, this is overwhelming. I mean, I knew I was pregnant; I think I was avoiding actually *thinking* about any of this.

Damn. I'm having a baby.

"You need to get plenty of rest. Drink lots of water." Dr. McCormick is still reeling off things for me to do.

"Sure. Yeah. I know." Rest? What's that? I'm up at three every morning to get to the bakery. I work ten- to twelve-hour days. I can't just stop doing that; I've got a business to run. I'll just have to figure it out.

"I'll make sure she does what she needs to do, Sam."

I watch as both men stand up, shake hands, and smile at each other like they're already in a bromance. *Ugh.* I slowly stand and turn toward the door. "*I'll* do what I need to do, Doc. Thanks for everything."

I'm out the door and through reception when I hear my name. I keep moving. I know he'll catch up, but I need to keep walking. I move past his car and over to a shady area near a tree. Once I get there, I turn in a full circle, looking for... what? I don't know.

I start to veer left when I feel a hand on my upper arm. "Sadie?"

"Oh, shit." The tears have come out of nowhere. Just, *bam*, tears. I pull my arm away from his hand and start to walk again.

"Sadie. It's going to be okay."

Charlie is walking next to me, but I'm not looking his way. I need to get the hell out of here.

"How do you know?" I say loud enough for him to hear.

"Honey, stop. Please."

Honey? He used the same endearment that night on the cruise. That and many others—some more sexy than sweet. I remember it all. Hell, I've thought about it numerous times over the last two months. I've needed to think about something happy. Sometimes at night, when I'm lying alone in my bed, my mind goes back to that night. I laugh aloud as I muse whether sex with Charlie changed my life. Now that I'm carrying his child, I can no longer muse. Sex with him was indeed life-changing.

I halt in my steps. Why isn't he reacting to this news? Good or bad? It's like he cares, but doesn't, if that makes any sense. All he's done is make sure I'm okay. He's not said one word about our child. *Our* child.

I rotate until I'm facing him. "This is life-altering news, Charlie. I'm pregnant, and you haven't said word one about that fact. You're going to be a father, and we barely know each other. What's supposed to happen now? Are you just going to visit from time to time? Because I'm not moving away. I've got a business to run, and my entire family—"

Oh, shit buckets. My family. The sobs start up again, and it's not pretty. My dad, Lainie, Agatha, Violet, and Keely. They'll all need to know. I'll have to call a family meeting—do it all at once. That's the only way to ensure they all hear it from me, because once one of them knows, it'll spread like wildfire. How will they react? I know, deep down, they'll all be happy about the newest Palmer, but worry will show on each of their faces. They've been concerned about me ever since my breakup with Andrew. And for good reason. The man is an asshole. He spent the entire week I was on the cruise harassing each and every one of them. They had no idea he'd cheated on me until I sent them that text message. I had to be the one to describe, in vivid detail, what he did with Candy in *my* bed.

It didn't end when I returned either. He showed up daily at the bakery wanting to talk to me. Then, he started showing up asking to see my books. *What the fuck?* Of course I denied him that, because he has no stake in my business. None. Well, he has one. He owns the building. Or I should say, his mother owns the building, and for some reason he feels he's got some sort of rights to my business, which is complete bullshit. Leasing a building to me doesn't give them jurisdiction over the business. At least I hope not. I haven't read the entire lease nor have I hired an attorney. I need to do that soon, though.

"Sadie?"

I'm drawn from my internal rant by a deep voice. And warm hands. One each on my upper arms. They're moving down to my wrists, where he runs a soothing thumb over each pulse point. If he's trying to calm me down, it's working. I blink up at him.

"I'm not sorry you're pregnant. I've always wanted a family."

"B-b-but you don't even know me."

"Then I'll get to know you. And you'll get to know me. We've got time. Come on, let's sit. Get you off your feet." He pulls me over to a park bench that I've never noticed before.

CHAPTER THIRTEEN

Charlie

I'VE LOST HER. No, she's not dead. She did try to run away, but I was able to get her to sit long enough to calm herself. Now we're both sitting on a bench beneath a tree, and I've got my arm lying across her shoulders. She's been crying since we left the doctor's office, but nothing I've said so far has been enough to quiet her. I'm at a loss what to do right now. Ordinarily, I'd call my sister for advice, but while she's my confidante, she's also a loudmouth. The last thing I need is for my entire family to get involved in this. And that's what would happen. Everyone would jump on the family jet and descend on Page, Arizona, like locusts in a matter of hours. The thought makes me laugh.

"What's so funny?" she asks through sniffles.

"I was thinking about Laura."

"What about her?" I feel her wipe her nose on my dress shirt, but I couldn't care less.

"She'll be thrilled with the news. As will Catherine."

"Your sister?"

"The one and only."

"She'd be happy? But not your m-mom?"

I'm not sure what happened just then, but her question made her sobbing start again.

"I'm sure my mother will be happy. Eventually. She's rather vain. I'm not sure she'll appreciate the grandmother moniker just yet." I chuckle, but it's forced, because the thought of *Grandmother* Emily Ashbury will not go over well. I'm positive Laura and Catherine will be thrilled with the news. The rest of them? Not so much. But no matter; this is my life. I'm certainly old enough to make my own choices. As long as Laura's in my corner, it'll be fine.

"My m-mom is d-dead," she says between hiccupping sobs.

"Oh. I'm so sorry." I run my palm up and down her arm to soothe her. It helped before.

"Ovarian cancer when I was s-seven."

"Oh, baby," I coo. Dammit, that's sad. "I'm so sorry."

"Me too. *She'd* have loved to be a grandma. I know it."

"If she was anything like you, then I'm sure she was a wonderful mom."

Oh shit. That really did it. Her sobs are so loud we're getting looks from people leaving the doctor's office. But who cares?

"Really? You really think so?"

"I do. I know we don't know much about each other, but from the little I know, I'm positive you'll be an amazing mother."

"Th-thank you, Charlie," she says softly. "What about you?"

"What about me?"

"You didn't come here expecting to be a father."

"No."

There's a long pause. She's waiting for me.

"I'm not unhappy about it. Like I said, I've always wanted a child or two." Or five. "We haven't done this in the traditional order, but that's okay. We can remedy that."

"Remedy what?" Sadie pulls her head away from my chest quickly. She's still close enough for me to see the tears stuck to her lashes. Instead of crying now, she looks defiant.

"Us."

"Us? What do you mean, us?"

"I came here to see if what I felt on the cruise was real or if I was just living a fantasy. Now that I'm here and you're pregnant, I consider it a sign, of sorts. I want to see—"

"See what?" Sadie's scooted away from me.

"I want a relationship with you."

"Oh, shit," she mutters as she pushes herself to standing. "Charlie. You've no idea what you're talking about. Yes, our night together was mind-blowing. And it resulted in this," she says, placing her hand over her belly. "But I just got out of a six-year relationship. One that has turned into utter shit since I got back from the cruise."

"Wait. You were in a relationship on the cruise?"

"No." Sadie runs her fingers over the top of her head. Pulling out her hair tie, she runs her fingers through her hair. I watch as she twists it all up into a knotted chignon at the nape of her neck. "It's a long story."

"I've got time."

"Well, I don't. I need to get back to the bakery."

I move to stand. "That's fine. We'll stop by the pharmacy to get your prenatal vitamins and folic acid. I'll stock you up on bottled water. But tonight, you and I are going to sit down and talk. You'll have ample time to tell me your *long* story."

"Fine." She sighs, wiping away any remaining wetness on her face. "Let's go. I've already been gone too long."

We ride in silence to a pharmacy that sits only a block from the bakery, and we're still silent when we walk into the small shop. Fortunately, the aisle that holds the vitamins has what we need in stock. With those in hand, I find a twenty-four pack of bottled water and purchase that as well. When we exit the store, Sadie turns left and begins to walk away from me. Choosing my battles, I hop into my car and drive to her store. As I open my car door, I watch her walk toward me. Her head is down. She's either lost in thought or she's ignoring me. It doesn't matter which; I'm not going anywhere.

I take her vitamins and water in hand and enter the store first. Inside, I see the shop is still relatively busy. Two women are sitting at one of the small round tables near the window. Next to Polly, a tall woman is helping a petite blonde. There's quiet chatter going on around me. I set the bottled water on an empty spot on the counter and place the bag with Sadie's vitamins on top.

"How is she?" asks Polly.

"Dehydrated." I tap my hand on top of the package of water. "She needs to drink this."

"What's in the bag?" Polly nods toward the bag on the counter.

My God, the woman is nosey. "Prenatal vitamins and folic acid."

"For Sadie?" asks the tall redhead behind the counter.

I nod just as the bell above the door chimes and Sadie walks through.

"Prenatal vitamins?" I turn to see the petite blonde gaping at Sadie. "Sades? Prenatal vitamins?" Her question comes out in a screech.

I look back at Sadie, who is now glaring at me. "What the fuck, Charlie? Did you tell everyone in here I'm pregnant?" Now it's Sadie screeching. "You walked into *my* business and announced it to everyone here?" Okay, she's definitely angry.

"I didn't—"

"Those are *my* sisters," she says, pointing to someone behind me. "You had no right to tell anyone. I"—she jabs herself in the chest—"should have been the one to tell my *sisters*." She spits out the word sisters. "It's not your fucking place, Charlie." Running a palm over her face, she stops and glares some more. "This is a small town, Charlie. You just announced to the world that I'm fucking knocked up. Where do you get off? It's not your place. It's none of your goddamn business."

"Well, I beg—"

"Sadie?" comes a male voice emerging from the back room.

"Oh, great!" Sadie shouts. "This is fucking perfect. Andrew, what are you doing here?"

"You're pregnant?"

"Jesus," Sadie shouts. "I asked you a question. What are you doing here, Andrew?"

"Is it mine?" the short red-haired man asks, ignoring Sadie's demands.

Without responding to his question, she repeats, "Andrew? I've told you multiple times. Get the fuck out of my bakery."

Who the hell is Andrew?

Whoever he is, he makes the unfortunate mistake of not listening. "It's my investment."

"The fuck it is!" Sadie yells so loudly I feel an urge to cover my ears, but I don't. I need to hear this. "This place," she says pointing to the ground, "is mine." Next, she places a palm on her chest. Her breathing is labored. Her face flushed. I watch as her eyes start to glisten.

"Well, actually...," the idiot begins.

"Get out," Sadie says hoarsely. She looks at me. "You too, Charlie."

Me? What'd I do? Oh, right, I informed everyone in the shop that she's taking prenatal vitamins. I can see now why that was the wrong thing to do.

I watch, in slow motion, as Sadie's face turns so pale that it's nearly ghost white. I've seen that before. Sure, it was a three-hundred-pound defensive lineman, but when people faint, the look is the same. I move quickly just as she starts her descent. I can't let her hit the ground. The floor is concrete. If she hits her head, it could be catastrophic. I lunge for her and am able to get there in time. With my arms around her, I pull her toward me as I fall back onto the ground. Sure, I hit my head on the concrete, but I've got a thick skull.

"Sadie!" I hear more than one voice shout.

"Oh, shit. Sades?" It's the blonde woman. One of her sisters, I assume. She's at her side, concern covering her face. "Sadie?" she whimpers.

She's out cold. This entire episode here is my doing, but I'll worry about that later. "Place your hand beneath her head for me so I can get out from under her. I don't want her to hit her head."

"Okay," says the now weeping blonde. "Vi? Can you get my jacket? I want to put it under her head."

The tall redhead races into the back room and brings a small pillow with her. "It's from Sadie's office," she says, handing it to me. I place it on the ground. As gingerly as possible, I scoot out from beneath her and rest her head on the pillow. "Is there a blanket?"

"Sure." The tall woman runs back and returns in seconds, asking, "Should we call nine-one-one?"

"Let's give her a few minutes. Cold compress?" I ask no one in particular.

Before I know it, I've got a cool cloth in my hand. "Sadie? Honey?" I whisper as I gently place the cloth on her forehead. She's warm, but I attribute that to the stressful events that just occurred. She'd gotten herself worked up. Couple that with dehydration, and we get the perfect storm.

"Who are you?" asks the blonde who is now running her hand over Sadie's head.

"I'm Charlie."

"I know that. *Who* are you?"

"I'm...." I pause. "I'm Sadie's." And in that moment, that very moment, I know I mean it. I'm Sadie's, and she's mine. She just doesn't know it yet.

"He's from the cruise." This time Polly is answering. "Charlie? Is she going to be okay?"

I start to respond just as Sadie mumbles, "Yes. I'm fine." Her eyes flutter open. She attempts to sit up, but both the blonde and I hold her back.

"Sit still," I grunt. She can't move too quickly.

And she does.

"God, Sadie. You scared the fuck out of us," says the blonde beside me.

"Sorry."

"So, this guy is your cruise hookup?" The blonde points her thumb at me.

"Charlie, this is my baby sister, Keely." She points to the tall redhead. "And that's her twin, Violet."

Twins. Interesting. They look nothing alike, but that's not uncommon. "Nice to meet you two." I look down at Sadie. "I'm sorry I divulged your secret. I didn't mean to do that."

Sadie looks into my eyes. A lone tear slides out, and it breaks my fucking heart. I reach out and remove it with my finger. "Oh, angel. It's going to be okay. I've got you."

"So." The asshole, Andrew, has the gall to say, "Is the kid mine, Sadie?"

"Fuck off, Andrew," snaps Keely.

"Rude," he mutters. Turning his eyes back to Sadie, he snaps. "Is it?"

"No, it's mine. And I believe the lady asked you to leave."

"She asked you to leave too, dickhead," Andrew spits out.

"Yeah, well, I'm not going anywhere."

Andrew stands defiantly, arms crossed over his narrow chest. "Well, if you're not, I'm not—"

"Dude," interrupts Keely. "Get out before I kick your ass."

"I'd like to see you try."

Keely sits back on her heels. "I'll make one phone call, dick-breath, and you'll be hauled off for trespassing. Don't make me do it."

I don't look at Andrew but whatever she just said must do the trick because he snaps, "Fine. I'll go, but I'll be back." There's a pause. "With *Mother*."

Sadie groans, but it's apparently not in pain. "God. Not his mother," she says under her breath.

CHAPTER FOURTEEN

SADIE

HOW DID I GET HERE? No, I'm not talking existentially. I mean, how did I end up flat on my back on my bakery floor with five sets of eyes staring down at me? Well, six sets if you count Andrew, but his don't last long so there's five. When the bell above my door chimes, I sigh. "Is he gone?"

"Yes," says Violet softly. "He's been here for an hour. He was starting to get on my last nerve."

That makes me laugh. Not because he's annoying Violet, but because Violet finds him annoying. Usually nothing seems to bother her. I'm not the only one laughing. Keely has started to giggle, as had Polly. Charlie's the only one looking like his cat just died. He looks worried. Sincerely worried. And that concerns me. If Dr. Charles Ashbury is worried, I should be too.

"Am I going to be okay, Charlie?"

"Yes," he says calmly. "You're dehydrated, and that episode

a few minutes ago escalated quickly. We need to keep your stress levels down at least until you rehydrate and the morning sickness dissipates. Have you eaten lately?"

Have I eaten? When was the last time I ate? I can't remember.

"No, she hasn't eaten," informs Polly. "What about a cupcake?"

"Sugar would help her in the short term, but she'll just crash in no time. She needs real food."

"I'll make her some pancakes." That's Violet. "Does that sound good, Sadie?"

I nod. It really does sound good. "Sure, thanks, Vi."

"Do you have somewhere you could lie down? In your office, perhaps?"

"Yes. I have a small sofa." I start to push myself up to sitting, but I'm dizzy. Before I can do a thing, Charlie has one arm beneath my knees, the other behind my back, and he's dead lifting me. "No!" I shout. "Your back!"

"Shh. I've got you." Looking at Polly, he asks, "Where's her office?"

Keely jumps in. "Follow me, hot stuff."

I giggle, because, God, my sister is so funny.

In minutes, I'm on my little couch, pillow beneath my head and my throw over my legs. I'm suddenly exhausted. Well, not suddenly, but pretty close. It hits me like a ton of bricks. When Violet presents me with three blueberry pancakes, it actually smells good. It tastes even better. I eat quickly while drinking one full bottle of water. When that's gone, I'm presented with a second one. "Drink up, Sadie," says a bossy Charles.

"Fine." I take the bottle and drink it too. It's surprising how much better I feel already. Lying back on the small pillow, I close my eyes, and that's it. I'm out.

I WAKE TO WHISPERING. I continue to feign sleep so I can hear what Keely and Violet are saying.

"No. You need to let him take care of her," whisper-hisses Keely.

"But we don't even know him." Violet sounds distressed.

"Well, *she* knows him. Biblically. That's his baby in there. He wants to do it. We need to let him do it."

"I just think—"

"Look, Vi. Do you want him to resent us?"

"Of course not. But—"

"Because you know what happens if he resents us?" Keely doesn't give poor Violet a chance to respond. "He'll keep us from Sadie *and* the baby. Do you want that?"

"No," Violet says, shocked. "He wouldn't—"

"She's right, Keels. He'd never do that."

She turns to me like she knew I was listening. "How can you be so sure?"

I blink at the ceiling, then look at my baby sisters. "I don't know him very well, but I know he'd never do that." I look around my tiny office. "Where is he?"

"He said he had to run some errands."

Errands? Sitting up too quickly, I feel a wave of nausea hit me. "What time is it?"

"It's after five."

Shit. "I need to get prep done for tomorrow." I move to my feet and halt my movements. I'm going to lose whatever's in my stomach. Slapping my hand over my mouth, I race out the door to the bathroom, but I don't make it this time.

"Gross, Sades," gurgles Keely.

"Move please, Keely. I'll take care of it," Violet says, rolling her eyes.

"I can do it," Keely chuffs. "I was just saying—"

"You can both head home. I've got this," says a deep voice from somewhere behind me.

Wiping my mouth after rinsing it in the sink, I turn to all three of them. "*I've* got this. You *three* need to go home."

CHAPTER FIFTEEN

Charlie

THIS WOMAN... I know her. Well, I mean I know women like her. Laura for one. My mother for another. And what I've learned from them is 1) most of the time their defiance is only bluster, and 2) not to poke the bear. Sadie says she wants me to leave, but I prefer to believe she needs me. So that's why I ignore Sadie. "I've got this," I say, smiling at Keely and Violet.

"Fine," grumbles Keely.

"Sadie?" asks a nervous Violet.

"I'm fine. You two go home. Be sure you update Aggie and Lainie. I'm sure you guys have already blabbed." She pauses at the bathroom door. "Did you tell Dad?"

"No. Lainie told us to keep it to ourselves. That you should tell him."

See? I knew they'd blab. "Thanks. I'd like to tell him myself."

"Call if you need anything, Sadie," says Violet, softly

adding, "Oh, and everything is ready to go for tomorrow. Also, Agatha is coming in to replace you for a few days until you feel better."

"Vi!" Sadie whines. "I can work."

Keely interrupts. "No, you can't. Charlie said you need to rest for a few days. So that's what you're going to do."

"Keels, I'm fine. I can work."

"No, Sadie," Violet says, piling on.

It's my turn to jump into the fray. "Let's get you on track with your fluids and vitamins. You'll feel better after a day or two of rest."

She glares at me from her spot inside the bathroom. "I'm only listening to you because you're a doctor. If you were just a normal, average guy, I'd tell you to take a hike."

I chuckle, thinking she's kidding. From the look on her face, I'd say she isn't. Clearing my throat, I ask Sadie, "I'm ready to go when you are. Do you need to take anything with you?"

"My purse, my laptop. Oh, and my lease."

I help her gather her things, carrying them out myself. I lead her to my car, but she veers off toward the back of the store. "Sadie? My car is over here."

"And mine is back here." She points to a small parking lot behind the bakery.

"Sadie?"

"I'm fine. I'll see you later, Charlie."

Oh, now this is humorous. She thinks she's just going home alone? "Come here, Sadie," I say in my bossy voice.

Sadie stops midstep, turning to face me. I see a deep pink blush on her face. *She remembers.* Without a word, she begins to walk toward me. When she's close enough to touch, I say, "You're staying with me. Keely has agreed to pack a bag for you and bring it to my hotel."

"No. I—"

"Yes," I say simply, confidently.

"Fine." She huffs. "But I want my own room."

"No."

"Come on, Charlie." She's whining again.

"I've got a suite. Plenty of room." Only one bedroom, but she'll see that once we get there.

Sadie rolls her eyes at me, and it's adorable. Taking her hand in mine, I lead her back to my car.

"Keely said your car would be fine here."

"It will be."

Can a person sound like Eeyore? If so, Sadie just did.

CHAPTER SIXTEEN

SADIE

HIS SUITE HAS ONLY one bedroom. I should have known. He was right about the size of the place, though. It's bigger than my entire apartment by half. There's a small kitchen, a living area with a television mounted above a gas fireplace, a dining area, and two full bathrooms. Thank goodness for that.

I watch as he sets my laptop, purse, and files on a small desk nestled in a corner. There's a large window next to it that gives me a perfect view of Lake Powell off in the distance. I love Lake Powell. It was one of my mom's favorite places, so it holds special meaning in my heart. Plus, my sister Agatha got engaged up there with all of us in attendance, which makes it doubly sentimental.

I watch as he moves about the room. Every once in a while, he glances at me shyly. It's sort of sweet. Sort of. It'd be sweet and romantic if this entire day hadn't been one clusterfuck after another. I take in a huge gulp of air and release it. "I need to call my dad."

He steps over to the desk and then back to me, holding something in his hand. "Your phone."

I take it and look around for somewhere private.

"The bedroom has a door if you'd like some privacy."

I would. I walk into the bedroom, shut the door, and sit on the edge of the bed. Staring down at my cell, I do my best to focus on my words. *Dad, hey, guess what? I'm preggers.* No, that's not good. *Dad? Hi. It's me, Sadie. You'll never guess what happened....* Nope. Still not right. I just need to do it fast. Like ripping off a bandage. I click on my contacts and touch Dad's name.

"Hello?"

"Daddy?" Oh, crap. I dug out the *daddy.* He's going to know....

"What's wrong, Sadie?"

See?

"Nothing. Um, it's just... I've got something to tell you."

"Are you okay?"

"Yes. No." I pause because ripping off the bandage doesn't seem to be working. "I'm... I'm...."

Just do it, Sadie.

"Dad, I'm pregnant."

Silence. It's true what they say—it's deafening. "Dad?"

"Pregnant?"

"Yes."

"Does Andrew know?"

"Yes, but—"

"Does this mean I'm going to have to be nice to that fucking tool?"

I release a nervous giggle. My dad doesn't cuss. Well, not

much. According to him, he uses it when absolutely necessary. "No, you don't have to be nice to him." I need to tell him but, God, what's he going to think of me?

"The baby..." *I can do this.* "...isn't Andrew's."

I hear a loud sigh of relief through the telephone. "Thank fuck."

I laugh again, and this time it comes from deep within my chest. Relief comes with it. "Do you want to know who the father is?"

"Is he local?"

Local? That's a difficult question to answer. He's in the other room, but I'm not going to say that. "Yes and no." I'll explain the fact that he's not going to be local forever.

"Bring him by for dinner tonight."

"Dad, it's already six."

"Bring him by for dinner tonight. See you in an hour." I hear the phone click, and that's the first time my dad has ever hung up on me, ever. So, okay, he didn't really hang up on me, but he did end the call abruptly. He probably didn't want to hear me attempt to negotiate. Fine.

I stand up too quickly and dizziness overtakes me, so I sit back down on the bed. Then I scoot back until my head is on one heck-of-a-plush pillow. Holding the phone up, I hit redial.

"Sadie? You're not backing out on me—"

"Daddy, can you come to me? I'm not feeling the best...."

His bossy tone turns sugary sweet in milliseconds. "Of course, honey. I'll be right over."

Before he can hang up, I'm able to say, "I'm at the hotel. Room 682." I don't need to tell him which hotel. There's only one in Page, Arizona.

"Why are you at the hotel?"

"That's where Charlie is staying."

"The father?"

"Yes."

"I'll be there in half an hour."

"Thanks, Daddy," I say sleepily. "Love you."

"Love you more."

CHAPTER SEVENTEEN

Charlie

WHEN I HEAR the knock on the door, I assume it's room service. I ordered a selection of entrees for Sadie, since I'm not sure what she'll feel like eating. But, when I open the door, it's not room service. It's a man, about my father's age. "Yes?"

"I'm here to see Sadie, son."

"Is she expecting you?" I mean, she said nothing to me, but then again, she fell asleep, so we haven't spoken for a while. I didn't want to intrude on her alone time, but I started to worry after twenty minutes of no Sadie. I assumed she needed rest after everything that happened today, so I let her sleep.

"Yes. She called. Asked me to come to room 682. So, here I am." The man steps through and I can't help noticing his size. He's as tall as I am, so about six foot two, and nearly as broad across the shoulders. In his heyday, he was most likely bigger than I am today.

"You're...?"

"Sadie's father. Rob. Rob Palmer."

He holds his hand out, and I take it. "Nice to meet you, Mr. Palmer. I'm Charles Ashbury. Call me Charlie."

"Call me Rob."

I watch as he walks toward the sitting area and plops down onto the one and only side chair. "Can I get you anything?"

"My daughter."

"Right." I've turned to make my way to the bedroom when I hear another knock. That's got to be my room service.

I hear the knock again, but this time it sounds more urgent.

"That'd be the rest of them," says Rob as he leans forward to remove his leather jacket.

The rest of them? The knocks are getting more insistent, so I increase my pace. I pull the door open and must look surprised, because the tiny blonde woman from earlier starts to laugh, loudly. "Told you he'd be surprised."

Keely leads the way into the hotel room, followed closely by Violet. After that, I've no clue who is coming in until they start introducing themselves. With my hand out, I shake hands one at a time.

"Charlie. Nice to meet you. I'm Lainie, Sadie's oldest sister." The curvy brunette steps past me, giving me a warm smile, all the while rubbing circles over her abdomen. Is she pregnant too?

Lainie. I say her name in my head, hoping I'll remember it.

"Keeton. I'm Lainie's," grumbles a huge guy in a leather jacket and jeans. Remind me not to mess with that guy. I raise my hand to shake his but can't because they're filled with box after box of pizza. Pizza that smells delicious.

Keeton.

"Hi, Charlie. I'm Agatha, and this is my fiancé, Ian."

"Ex-FBI," murmurs the lanky Ian.

I know why he said it. It's a threat, but he smiled as he said it, so that's good, right?

Agatha and Ian.

Unsure if that was the last of them, I step out into the hallway and look left and right. When no one is in sight, I walk back into the room and let the door shut on its own.

When I look up, I see my living area filled to the brim with Sadie's family. I move toward the bedroom. "Let me wake Sadie."

"No."

I look over, not sure who said that. "No?"

"Let's get to know each other." I see the speaker this time. It's the curvy, pregnant sister, Lainie.

"So, Charlie," she says with a reassuring smile, "I believe we've established that Sadie is two months pregnant and you're the father. Correct?"

"Correct." Here we go. I wouldn't be surprised if one of them asks me what my intentions are.

The next question comes from the sister with the FBI agent fiancé, Agatha. With her hand on her own chest she says, "I'm Agatha. Now. You met my sister on the cruise?"

"Yes. We met on the cruise."

"Where are you from?"

Ah, I know who asked me that. Violet. "Boston."

"Boston?" asks Agatha. I watch as she pulls out a notebook and pen. Shit. Is she going to investigate me? It's okay. I've got nothing to hide. I watch as Ian leans over and whispers something in her ear.

This is getting damn serious.

"You're a doctor. We established that earlier. But what *kind* of doctor?" Keely is looking at me with one brow arched. What is she expecting? A medical examiner?

"I'm an orthopedic surgeon." I go ahead and explain my

work because I know that's coming next. So, I repeat, verbatim, the same thing I said to Sadie earlier today. "I deal with the musculoskeletal system. Specifically, my area relates to sports medicine. I treat athletes who've suffered season-ending and sometimes career-ending injuries."

"Wow, I bet that means you can't leave Boston, because you're some fancy-ass doc, huh?"

"Keely, I don't have a brick and mortar practice. I have privileges at hospitals all over the country. I tend to travel to the patient, since I work almost exclusively with professional athletes."

"Hm." Keely's voice sounds almost like a scoff. "Okay. So, you could live anywhere?"

"I could."

"But, will you?" asks Lainie. "Sadie does have a brick and mortar business to run. She can't just move to Boston."

"And she's not going to want her baby gone half the year. I think you need to consider all of those things," adds Violet softly.

Wow, this group is tough. "Frankly, guys, that's between Sadie and me."

"Why'd you come here?" asks the gruff-looking biker dude.

"For Sadie."

"Explain." Biker dude doesn't waste words.

So, I explain. I tell them as much as I can without being too graphic. I tell them I tried to find Rachel Montgomery with no luck. That I'd searched for her for two months. When I mentioned the name she used on the ship, I heard several *oohs* and *ahs*. Then I tell them about the T-shirt. Several of them laugh. I'm not sure which ones. Damn, this is overwhelming.

When I'm done, Rob is the one to speak. He stands and moves toward me. "Son?"

"Yes, sir."

"It's not going to be easy."

What's he talking about?

"That asshole, Andrew, hurt her something fierce."

I nod but it's only to encourage him to keep talking. I don't know the story about Andrew, other than the one I witnessed at the bakery.

"He's still messing with her, Dad," mutters Keely. "Let's get Keeton to kick his ass."

Keeton grunts and nods. "My pleasure. The guy is a dick."

So, I guess that means he's willing to beat up the unsuspecting Andrew. Good to know.

"No violence," Lainie states quickly. "Dad's right, Charlie. Sadie's been through a lot and is still dealing with Andrew."

I saw that firsthand.

"She's a tough nut to crack, Charlie," says Rob. "She's got armor around her heart. Ever since her mom passed."

"I can see that."

"We'd better leave it at that. Let's all agree to give Charlie a chance, yeah?" Rob has turned to face the group.

Some nod in agreement, some say, "Agreed."

I guess that means I've passed the initial round of questioning from the Palmers. Good. Attempting to change the subject, I quickly say, "Let me get Sadie."

As I step toward the bedroom, another knock sounds. *That's my room service. I hope.* As I turn to get that, Keely jumps up. "I got it, hot stuff. Go get Sadie."

So I do as I'm told.

Shit. *What just happened?*

CHAPTER EIGHTEEN

SADIE

"SADIE?"

I feel my body being gently jostled.

"Sadie? Wake up. You have company."

My eyes open slowly. I don't ever remember being this tired before. Exhausted doesn't seem to cover my aching muscles and headache. My lashes flutter a few times until I get my bearings. I peek around me and remember—I'm not at home in my own bed. I'm in Charlie's hotel room. What'd he just say? "Someone's here to see me?"

Who? Oh, shit. Dad. I sit up too quickly, and dizziness strikes again. Luckily, I don't feel any nausea this time. "Dad?"

"Your father is here, yes. Among others."

I glance up into Charlie's pretty eyes. He looks... what? Irritated? Worried? Oh, shit, I can't fret about that now. I'll figure it out later. Scooting off the side of the bed, I stand slowly. "Sorry. I called him and invited him here, then fell asleep."

The look, whatever it was, is replaced by a smile. "No problem, Sadie. I just wasn't prepared to meet your... all of them."

"All of them?" Oh, shit. They didn't....

I stand up and run my fingers through my hair. It needs to be redone. Hell, I need a long, hot shower, but that'll have to wait. Apparently, they've staged an intervention or something close to that. Out in the living area, I blink several times. Yep, they're all here. Even Keeton and Ian, my soon-to-be brothers-in-law.

"Sadie." Dad stands up and hurries toward me.

When I'm wrapped up in his strong arms, I feel tears burn the back of my eyes. "Hi, Daddy," I whisper.

"Hi, sweetie." Stepping back, he looks into my eyes. "Not feeling well? Morning sickness?"

I nod.

"Your mother had morning sickness something terrible with all four pregnancies."

"Great," I mutter.

"Rachel's only lasted the first three months, as I recall. It was smooth sailing after that."

I look over at Charlie as he arches one brow. Now he knows where the name Rachel came from.

"One month to go. Yay," I cheer weakly. Why do I feel so weak? I turn away from Dad to find a seat on the sofa between Agatha and Lainie. I tap Lainie's growing tummy absently. I can't help it. She's so cute pregnant.

"Sadie?" Charlie asks tentatively. "I ordered room service, and it appears there's pizza as well. You need to eat. And drink." Charlie walks over to the kitchen area. Opening his small fridge, he pulls out a bottle of water. "Would anyone like something to drink?"

When he's bombarded with every voice in the room at once with their drink orders, he points to the fridge. "Help yourself."

For some reason, that makes me laugh. Charlie's only been around my family for a short time, and he's already figured out they should get their own shit.

My stomach growls. I look at Lainie. "I guess I'm hungry."

"I bet. You haven't eaten since you had pancakes earlier," says Charlie as he hands me my bottled water.

He points to the pizza box and looks at Keeton. "May I?"

"Help yourself."

"Do you want pizza, honey?" he says, looking at me. Only me. "Or there's a grilled chicken sandwich and fries or a steak and baked potato, along with a chocolate malt."

"Wow. I'd definitely like the chocolate malt." I look at the open pizza box. I want pizza, but I have a feeling that Charlie really thought about what to order me. "Which one of the meals you ordered would be better for me?"

I'm taken aback by the smile. He's beaming at me. "Either one will be good. The bun on the grilled chicken sandwich is whole wheat, the fries are sweet potato. There's a small salad with each meal with lots of leafy vegetables. Which one sounds best to you?"

"You pick. Both sound yummy, Charlie. Thank you for being so considerate."

"Let's do this. I'll put all the food on the table, and you can pick out the things that sound the best to you. I'll eat whatever you don't want."

"Oh, that's so sweet. Thank you."

I watch Charlie move over to a cart filled with covered dishes. Smiling as he walks away, it's then I notice no one is talking, and that's saying something. The Palmer family is *never* quiet. I look to my left to see Lainie, Keely, and Keeton staring at me. On my right, the rest are doing the same. "What?"

"Whoa," mutters Keely.

"Exactly." Lainie nods as she pats me on my leg. Leaning closer, she whispers in my ear, "I like him."

I look over to see Charlie setting out all of the food, arranging it just so. And he's doing that for *me*. "You know what, Lain? I do too." I like him so much, it scares me.

AFTER EVERYONE FILES out of the hotel room, I sit quietly while Charlie picks up the place. My sisters stacked all the pizza boxes next to a trash can before they left, but the remains from room service are all over the place. When I spy a glass over on a side table, I stand and walk to it.

"Nope. Sit. I've got it."

"I'm not an invalid, Charlie. I can help." I want to help.

"Sweetheart, let me do this." The look on his face is unreadable. He doesn't look angry, but he also doesn't look happy. "Please?"

"Alright." I sit back down and start to twiddle my thumbs, literally. "I'm bored."

I hear him mumble something, but he's too quiet. I can't make out what he said.

"What?"

"Nothing."

"Charlie? Tell me."

I watch as he rolls the cart to the door, opens it, and rolls it outside in the hallway. He also gathers up the pizza boxes and sets them on top of the cart. "I'll call down to let them know they can pick this up."

I guess he's not going to tell me. *Passive-aggressive? Meet Charlie Ashbury. Oh, you've already met?*

Well, I don't need this. I think I'll shower. I look around the space for the suitcase my sister promised me and find it sitting behind the couch. Grasping the handle, I start to lift but Charlie's there instantly.

"Let me."

"Charlie." I release a frustrated sigh. "This isn't going to work if you think you have to do everything for me. I've been taking care of myself and a few others forever."

He leans close to me. So close I can smell his cologne. "Just give me this. Let me do the heavy lifting, literally."

I laugh, but it's not happy. "Are you going to come to the bakery and carry ingredients around for me? Huh?"

"If necessary. Yes."

I scoff. "You're kidding."

I watch as he runs his fingers through his hair, then over his face. He's frustrated. "Look. I'm tired, you're tired. Let's get a good night's sleep. We have all day tomorrow to talk. And we do need to talk, Sadie."

"Fine."

CHAPTER NINETEEN

Charlie

"FINE."

I'm really starting to hate that word. Sadie says it whenever she's irritated. Usually about something I've asked her. It's like she's holding back. Waiting for the right time to fight back. That's okay with me. Two can play at that game. "Fine. Let's go to bed."

I coax the suitcase out of the hand of the most stubborn woman I've ever met. Well, that's not true, but she's damn close. I carry it into the bedroom and place it on top of the luggage stand nearest the closet. I've started to unzip it when Sadie stops me.

"Seriously? I can unzip my own bag." I hear her mutter "Jesus" afterwards, but I choose to ignore her.

"Fine." Sitting on the bed, I watch Sadie unzip her bag.

Pulling it open, Sadie laughs. "That little...."

"What?"

Standing back, I see her bag is filled to the gills. There's a small striped bag on top that is probably toiletries. But below that looks like a pillow of chiffon. "What is all that?"

"Sexy underwear." Sadie laughs, and it's a nice sound. "All thanks to matchmaker Keely."

"Oh?" Wow, that piqued my interest. Except I prefer Sadie without underwear. Without anything. The woman is delectable. I stand to get a closer look, but she slams the lid shut.

"Nuh-uh, big guy. Stay out of my suitcase." I look at her hands and see items that look practical. Sleep pants and a few other things. "I'm going to shower. Do you want the bed or the couch?"

"The bed."

She looks surprised. "Oh, sure. Right. I'll take the couch."

"Sadie. We're both sleeping in the bed."

"No. That's not—"

"We're both sleeping in the bed." I use the bossiest tone in my arsenal.

"Okay. Right." She turns on her heel and strides into the bathroom.

"Damn straight," I mutter. I'm done sleeping alone. I thought I liked my solitude until I slept with Sadie. I haven't had a decent night's sleep for two months.

While she showers, I undress, hanging up my slacks and putting my dress shirt into my laundry bag. I do the same with my socks and undershirt, leaving me in only my boxer briefs. I unzip the luggage compartment that holds my sleepwear. I'd love to tell you I'm a free spirit as it relates to bed clothes, but I am not. The truth is, I enjoy the feel of freshly pressed cotton nightwear.

Before sliding into bed, I walk out to the main room to get three bottles of water. Two for Sadie, one for me. Setting hers on the nightstand on her side of the bed, I open mine and drink half of it. Sliding beneath the cool sheets, I sit up and rest my back against the headboard. Waiting. And waiting. And waiting some more. It's taking her too damn long in there. I slide out of bed and walk around to the bathroom door. I reach for the knob, but then I opt to knock first, softly.

"Yeah?" she says weakly.

"Sadie? May I come in?"

I hear the sounds of rustling and clanking of mystery items. "Yes."

I open the door and sweep the room with my eyes. Sadie is sitting on the toilet, towel wrapped around her body, but she's not wet.

"Honey? What's wrong?"

"I just got dizzy. Then I couldn't figure out how to turn on the stupid water. The shower is more complicated than a Rubik's Cube."

"It is, isn't it? It needs to come with a manual." I chuckle as I step into the large walk-in shower. Turning on the water, I set the temperature to warm, but not hot. I look back at her and see worry line her face.

Stepping back out, I hold out my hand. "Let me help."

"Charlie, I—"

"Let me."

When she stands, I tug on the towel around her. She lets it go, and I get a glimpse of her curvy form. I look down at her belly and don't yet see any sign of our baby growing inside her. Soon, though. I move to push down my sleep pants along with my boxers and stand before her, hard. What? It can't be helped. She does this to me. Next, I unbutton my sleep shirt and lay it on top of the pants.

Holding her hand, I pull her into the warm spray and direct her until she's facing me. I adjust the nozzles until she has one shower head hitting her lower back and the other raining down on her hair. "God, that feels so good," she moans, and my dick gets harder.

"I'm glad." I reach for the shampoo and rub it over my hands. Once her hair is wet enough, I start to work the shampoo at the crown of her head then down to the ends. Her hair is longer than I remember on the cruise. I look down and see her eyes are closed. She looks relaxed. "Feel good?"

"So good."

"Lean your head back. Let's rinse you off."

She does as I ask. Next, I squirt body soap into my palm and work it into a lather. Starting at her shoulders, I wash each arm above and below. Getting more soap, I do the same to her legs. I've been avoiding certain parts of her because I'm not sure what she wants. Turning her around, I wash her back and run soap over each of her luscious cheeks. She moans and pushes her bottom back just slightly.

"Sadie?"

"Don't stop, Charlie," she whispers.

I pump more soap into my palms and slide them around to her belly, concentrating on the spot that holds our child. I stop for a second, thinking about that. Leaning into her, I lower my head and whisper in her ear. "We made a life here." My palm is circling her abdomen.

"We did." Sadie's voice is so soft; if I weren't so close, I may have missed it.

Gathering up soap bubbles, I slide my palms slowly upward, stopping right below her breasts. I hesitate. This is new ground we're covering. I don't want her to feel like she has to do this.

I stop overthinking when I feel her hands over mine. She pushes mine up over her hard nipples. "Squeeze them, Charlie," she says breathlessly. "They're so sensitive."

I slide my palms back and forth over her. Her tips are as hard as glass. I pluck and play with them while kissing and sucking on her neck right below her ear. Her breathing is labored.

"Oh, God, Charlie. Don't stop. I think I'm about to come."

I've heard some women can come from nipple play alone, but I've never witnessed it firsthand. This is amazing. I pinch and tweak at each peak until I hear her. A moan so deep and rich I feel like I'm about to lose it myself.

I quickly turn her around and kiss her deeply. She kisses me back in a frenzy of tongue and teeth. Lifting her off the ground, I gently lean her against the tile, placing my dick at her entrance.

"Oh, shit. That's cold." She giggles.

"I'll warm you up," I say as I push my cock into her hard and fast. "Fuck. You feel so good, Sadie."

"Oh, my God, Charlie."

"Good?" I plunge into her again.

"Fuck, yes!" she shouts at the top of her lungs.

I look down and watch her breasts bounce with each thrust. She has beautiful breasts, but I can't help picturing how big they'll get during her pregnancy—how rotund and gorgeous she'll be. Hell, if she already makes me hard just with one look now, I can only imagine the effect she'll have on me when she's round with my child. Damn, that thought is all it takes. I come hard inside her. I feel like I'm emptying two months' worth into her womb.

Leaning my head in until our foreheads are touching, I say, "I knew you'd be my undoing." I kiss her nose then her lips softly. "I'm so glad I found you." And I mean that in every way possible.

WE CRAWL into bed after drying off. I watch as Sadie slips on clean, practical cotton panties, her sleep pants, and a Sadie Cakes Bakery tee. I opt to remain nude, which appears to trouble my girl.

"You're not going to put, erm, anything on?"

"I can. I prefer to wear pajamas." I slide out of bed to retrieve my nightclothes from the bathroom. Once I'm dressed, I stop before slipping into bed. "Do you need anything, my love?"

Her face turns a lovely shade of pink. "No. I'm good."

Once I'm tucked in, I remind her, "Please drink some of the water there." I point to her nightstand.

"Fine."

See? Frustrating woman. I roll toward her. She seems lost in thought.

"Sadie?"

Looking over at me, she gives me a soft smile. "Yeah?"

I hold my arm out. "Come here."

She rolls over to her side and scoots back until we're spooning. Her gorgeous bottom fits perfectly against me. Just like I remember. Wrapping my arm carefully around her, I whisper, "If my arm starts to bother you, or if you feel nauseous, let me know."

"I will."

I reach back to switch off the light, and we're covered in near darkness. A glow from the window is the only light in the room. We lie in silence for minutes, maybe longer. I don't want to go to sleep. I think I'm afraid I'll wake up and she'll be gone again. "Sadie?"

"Yeah?"

"Don't leave me."

She turns to face me. The light gives her face an ethereal glow. She furrows her brow.

"I don't want to wake up and find you gone again."

"I won't." Rolling over completely until we're face-to-face, she smiles, then kisses me. It's a sweet kiss. "Thank you for taking care of me today."

"I'll do it forever if you'll let me."

A small laugh escapes her. "You have no idea what you're promising. I'm not worth that kind of commitment, Charlie. *Obviously.*"

What the hell does that mean? I have no idea what to say to that. So I do the only thing I can do; I kiss her like I mean it, then I whisper in her ear, "You're worth it, Sadie."

"You don't even know me."

"No. Not yet. But if what happened here tonight, with your family showing up here to vet me, is any indication, I have a feeling you're worth all the time and effort it will take to know you. If you weren't special, important, worth it, tonight never would have happened. So I feel goddamn lucky. I get to be the man who takes care of you. Our child gets to have you and your adoring family in his or her life." I pause for effect. "Not to mention you own a bakery. I hit the jackpot."

I hear sniffles and a little laugh. "You're a romantic, aren't you, Charlie *Assberry?*"

I chuckle. "With you, yes."

"Just wait. You're not used to Palmer-level crazy. You'll change your mind."

"Nope." I pop the *p.* "Not gonna happen. You've met Laura, right?"

I hear her sniffles turn into more giggles. "True."

I run my hand up and down her back and let my palm rest on her bottom. The perfect spot. "Night, baby."

"Night, Charlie."

Wait. I forgot to ask. "Hey, Sadie?"

"Yeah?"

"Do you think Agatha is investigating me?" Surely not.

"Oh, yeah, I'm sure she is. Sorry. I should have warned you;

she's our resident sleuth. She works with Ian's cybersecurity firm sometimes. You've got nothing to worry about." She pauses. "Right?"

"Right."

"See? No worries. Night, Charlie."

"Night, honey."

CHAPTER TWENTY

SADIE

"I'M READY." Charlie says after finishing off his bowl of oatmeal and fresh fruit.

"Ready? For what?"

"To hear the story of Andrew."

Setting my cup of decaf (yuck) down onto the dainty porcelain saucer, I stare at him. "Which part?"

"All of it."

I start to tear off bits of my napkin and place them on the table. By the time I've made a mini mountain of scraps, I start. "We met in college. At a party. Almost seven years ago." I pick up my glass of juice and sip. "I was in culinary school, he was at Arizona State. We hit it off right away. I thought...."

"Thought?"

Clearing my throat, I say it. "I thought he was my person." I half expect Charlie to laugh but he doesn't.

"But he wasn't."

"No. I guess not." I shrug. "The cruise. He was going to propose on the cruise."

Charlie sets his cup down slowly. "Oh?"

"But the day before we were set to leave, I got off work early." I pause because I hate this part. "I got off early, and when I opened the door to my apartment, he was already there. In my bed. With my neighbor, Candy."

"He was in bed with your neighbor?"

"Well, they were using my bed." I chuckle dryly. "He was doing things to her without a condom. Something *we'd* never done. Then he—" I blush thinking about it. "He went down on her. Something he'd never done with me."

"Why not?" Charlie says defiantly.

"He said it was gross."

"Wow. What an idiot."

"I told him to leave. He did. He went over to Candy's place. I had my locks changed and then I took off for the airport."

"I see." Charlie is rubbing the side of his face. "You said you hadn't gotten your birth control shot. Were you...?"

"He wanted a family. I thought I'd surprise him with the news I hadn't updated my shot. I feel so stupid. He was always mocking Candy, calling her a white trash stripper, always bashing her lifestyle, her clothes, her—her everything."

"Do you still love him?"

"God, no. You know the saying, fool me once, shame on you, fool me twice...?"

He nods.

"Well, I believe that wholeheartedly."

"So why is he hanging around your bakery? Is he stalking you?"

"No." I scoff again. "He's still with Candy." I roll my eyes. "I bet his mother is having a cow about that." I know it hasn't been particularly nice for me. She still lives next door, so he's around a lot. He drives up from Sedona several times per week. I see his car parked in the lot when I leave for the bakery. Of course, I've run into both of them numerous times. It sucks. I need to move, but my lease isn't up for several months. Besides, where would I go?

"So why is he hanging out at your store?"

I stand up from the small table and walk to the desk to gather up the file I brought from the bakery. "His mother owns the building the bakery is in. I'm leasing it from her. But, for some reason," I say as I open the folder, "they're under the impression that they've got a stake in my company." Sitting back down at the table, I place the folder next to my plate. "I brought my lease and all the papers associated with the building with me to see if I can find anything out of the ordinary."

"May I?" he asks as he points to some of the papers. There are a least seventy pages to the thing.

I shrug. "Sure." Why not? He's probably used to contracts and other things. Maybe he'll see something I won't.

We sit in silence, each of us reading the lease agreement. So far, I've read nothing out of the ordinary. That's what I think, anyway.

"Have you been paying any profits to," he leans closer, "Beryl Winchester?"

"No. Just the lease payment."

"Are you sure?"

"Yes?"

"Who is your accountant? Or, I guess, who pays your bills related to the bakery?"

"I have a guy." I look through the papers until I find the contract with the bookkeeper. "Beryl recommended him to me." I hold up the card. "His name is Lance Yudd, C.P.A."

"Would you mind if I called Lance Yudd? I have a question for him. We'll do it right now, on speaker phone."

"Okaaaay." My stomach feels like it's doing cartwheels inside me.

Charlie picks up the paper with Mr. Yudd's name. When he finds the number, he dials. I hear, "Lance Yudd here. Speak."

Wow, that's really unprofessional.

"Yes, Mr. Yudd, my name is Charles Ashbury. I represent Ms. Sadie Palmer," Charlie says, sounding very official. I want to giggle but I don't.

"Represent her?"

"Yes."

Lance's voice sounds tentative. "How can I help you?"

"I'd prefer to meet in person with a few of my colleagues, but we can handle this initial consultation via telephone."

"Colleagues?"

"Can you tell me the total sum you've transferred into Beryl Winchester's account from Sadie Cakes Bakery?"

I hear Lance bluster. "Um, well...."

"I'm waiting, Mr. Yudd."

"It's on the up-and-up. She signed the document."

"Are you referring to my client, Sadie Palmer?"

"Yes."

"What document?"

"The one that made Beryl Winchester a silent partner."

"What?!" I screeched. "I did not."

"Is that you, Ms. Palmer?"

"Yes, it's me. And I'm here to tell you I signed no such thing."

I watch as Charlie slowly lifts up a piece of paper. One that was included in the large stack of paper.

My mouth is gaping. I'm shaking my head vehemently all the while silently saying, "No."

"I'm afraid so," says a cocky-sounding Lancy Yudd.

"I have a feeling this document was placed with the others to conceal its content. A subterfuge, if you will," says Charlie angrily. "Please inform Ms. Winchester we'll be in touch. With both of you."

"Wait!" shouts Lance. "I had nothing to do with that."

"I highly doubt that, Mr. Yudd. Good day."

Charlie hits the end button. Part of me wants to congratulate him for doing such a great job acting like an attorney. But, really, all I want to do is cry. Correction. Puke, then cry. In an attempt to find some levity, I say, "You sure know how to do the lawyer thing."

His face reddens slightly. Is he embarrassed?

"Well, that's because...."

My mouth falls open again. "You're an attorney too?"

He shrugs almost apologetically. "I don't practice, but I passed the bar, so I suppose you could say that."

"Wow. You must be *extra* smart."

He smirks. "Extra smart. I like that."

I place my palm on my stomach. "I hope our little peanut gets that from you."

Charlie intakes a gulp of air. "Wow. Our little peanut? I hope he or she gets everything from you."

I blush. I can't help. "Well, how 'bout 90 percent me and the rest is the extra smart part of you."

"Deal."

We sit and stare at each other, both of us smiling like idiots. That is until I remember. "What the hell have Andrew and Beryl been doing to me?"

"Scamming you, no doubt." He leans forward, placing his elbows on his knees. "Tell me something."

I remain silent. Waiting for his question.

"Why *didn't* you read the lease?"

I feel the color drain from my face. "I've been asking myself the same damn question and the honest truth is, I trusted him. I thought we were going to be married and that he was looking out for me. That he wanted the best for me just like I did him."

Charlie is looking at me with pity and I hate it.

"Look. It's what they do for a living and I'm a trusting fucking fool. So there. That's why I signed it. That and all I've ever wanted was my own bakery and it was happening and I didn't want anything to stop it from happening. But I learned my lesson, Charles." I snap his formal name and it's not fair of me. Calming myself down, I look at him. "I mean Charlie. I'll learn to be less trusting and I'll be extra careful the next time I get the opportunity to own a bakery again."

"Honey, you don't need to be less trusting. The fact that you believed in your partner is a good quality. This is all on Andrew and his mother. Speaking of which, do you know where Beryl lives?"

"Sedona." I scoff. "Laura probably lives next door to her."

"Doubtful."

"Oh, right. Laura's mega-loaded. Beryl is just sort of loaded."

"Did Beryl grow up in Sedona?"

"Born and raised. She's proud of that fact."

I watch him pick up his phone. Pressing a button, he hits the speaker button. When a voice I recognize answers, he says, "Laura?"

"Charlie? Did you find her?"

"He did," I say loud enough for her to hear.

"Rachel." Laura pauses. "I mean Sadie. How are you, my dear?"

"Good. You?"

"Excellent now that I've heard your voice. So, what have you two been up to?"

There's silence. I know he wants to tell her. "Go ahead," I whisper.

"Grandmother?"

"Oh, shit. I know it's serious when you break out the G-word. What?"

"We're going to have a baby."

"No. Fucking. Way," Laura deadpans. "Serious?"

I giggle because Laura's so funny. "Serious."

"I'll be there in twenty-four hours. Are you in Sedona?"

"Page."

"Oh, Page? I love it up there. I spent many a summer up at the lake." Then we hear Laura yelling for Gloria to pack her bags.

"Glo is packing me up."

I'd like to stop her, but why? I've missed her. She'll love my sisters, and they'll love her.

"Before we let you go," Charlie says, "do you know a Beryl Winchester?"

We hear Laura snort and cough on the other end of the line. "God, I haven't heard that name in years. Yes. She's a bitch on wheels. Why do you ask?"

I look at Charlie. "How would she know Beryl?"

"I grew up in Sedona, darling."

"*Ohhh*, I see."

"She used to be Bernice Green before she married Andrew Winchester, but she thought Bernice was too common, so she changed it when she turned eighteen."

"I had no idea."

"Why are you asking about that snobbish bore?"

"We'll tell you all about it when you get here, Laura," Charlie says. "Safe travels. See you soon. I'll text you my hotel information."

"Hotel? Why? I've got a place close to Lake Powell."

"You do?" Charlie looks surprised.

"It's out on Rainbow Road. I'll send you the address in a few. I'll meet you there."

"Thanks, Laura."

"No problem. See you soon."

CHAPTER TWENTY-ONE

Charlie

"EXPLAIN THAT TO ME."

"Which part?" I'd just hung up the phone with Laura when I looked over to see Sadie quite perplexed.

"All of it. Laura grew up in Sedona?"

"Born and raised in Arizona. She moved out to Boston when she married Charles Ashbury."

"So, Ashbury is her married name? What's her maiden name?"

I hesitate. Once she hears Laura's family name, who knows what she'll do? But I can't lie to her. "Storrance."

Sadie's mouth opens and closes, but no sound comes out. It reminds me of a fish. A very pretty fish.

"St-Storrance? As in Storrance Soup? The biggest soup company in all the world?"

I nod but keep my smile at bay. I'm still not sure what she'll do. "Yes. In all the world."

"So...." She stands up from the table and begins to pace. "You're like mega-rich?"

"No." Not yet. "That's Laura's money."

She rolls her eyes. "Semantics."

"In a way. I'm sure I'll inherit something, but I don't like to think of Laura not being around. I like her."

Sadie turns quickly. "I do too." Her voice is panicked. "I'd never judge you because you have money."

I chuckle. "Well, thanks."

"It's just...."

"What?"

She sounds sad when her shoulders slump and she says, "While I don't care about your money, it does give me pause. I don't want to feel indebted to you."

"What do you mean you'd feel indebted?"

She stares at me like I'm an idiot. "Financially indebted."

"I don't use money or think about money like that. I'm me. You're you." I reach out and place my palm on her stomach. "Our peanut is where our real wealth lies. I'm indebted to *you* for giving me this gift. You can't put a price on that."

"Oh, my God." Sadie's eyes begin to water, and I'm not sure what to do.

"What did I say?" I don't know what I said but I'll just go ahead and say, "I'm sorry."

"No." She sobs and wipes her nose with the back of her hand. She walks toward me and wraps her arms around my neck, hugging me so tightly I'm almost breathless. "Charlie. That...," she sniffles, "was the most amazing thing to say." She continues to cry while I hold her in my arms. Rubbing my palm up and down her back, I do my best to say calming things like, "It's okay," and "I've got you, baby." Things of that nature. It seems to work, because after several minutes (ten), she stops crying.

Leaning back from me, she looks down at me with red, puffy eyes. "I won't hold your money against you, Charlie. As long as you use it for good. Not for evil."

I suspect she's referring to Andrew and Beryl Winchester, but I don't want to mention their names right now. "Good. I'm glad."

AFTER AN EMOTIONAL MORNING, Sadie decided to take a nap. It's exactly what she needs right now. Fortunately, she hasn't had a bout of morning sickness yet. It could be due to a good night's sleep or the oatmeal she ate this morning. Only time will tell if rest and a healthy, nutritious diet will help her.

While she sleeps, I decide to send Laura a text elaborating on the situation with Beryl and Andrew. I had a feeling she'd know Beryl. Laura's family wealth had her rubbing elbows with everyone in Sedona and surrounding areas. When she finds out what Beryl has been doing to Sadie, she may blow a gasket, but hopefully she'll use *her* money for good, not evil. I chuckle at Sadie's earlier words.

After I send off the text, I take the opportunity to check my emails. I'm due in Los Angeles in two days to perform surgery on an NBA player. I'll need to let Sadie know. She'll need to get used to my schedule. I'm away from home several times per month for several days each trip. I only hope she's understanding of that. We can make this work here in Arizona if she's willing. God, I hope she's willing. I refuse to be away from my child and, if I'm lucky, my wife.

CHAPTER TWENTY-TWO

WHAT TIME IS IT? I remember lying down for a nap, but that was this morning. It's early evening now, if the light coming through the window is any indication. I reach for my phone to check the time. Five thirty. I slept the day away. The sad thing is, I think I could sleep more. But I'd better not. I need to find out what's going on. Sliding out of bed, I do my best to contain my hair. I have a feeling I've got a Flock of Seagulls thing going on. Look 'em up. You'll see what I'm talking about.

I quickly brush my teeth and freshen up in the bathroom before heading into the living area. This room is nice, but I miss my own home. Well, I don't miss running into Candy and the douchebag, but my things are there. No matter. This situation is temporary. I'm only doing this to appease my family, Polly, and, I suppose, Charlie.

I search the open space but see no sign of him. "Hm. Where'd you go, Charlie?" In the kitchen area, I grab a bottle of water and drink half of it down in no time. See? I'm doing what I'm told. I took my vitamins this morning with my oatmeal, so that's all good. Moving back into the living room, I spy a piece of paper on the round, glass coffee table.

Sadie,

I had some errands to run. Be back by six to take you to dinner. You choose the place.

Yours, Charlie

Yours? That's very sweet. I probably shouldn't read too much into it though. He didn't write the word *love*, after all. I check the time on my phone. I've got thirty minutes to get ready. I only hope Keely packed me something other than sexy lingerie.

"YOU LOOK LOVELY, SADIE." Luckily, Keely did, in fact, put a dress in my suitcase. It's a wrap dress that dips very low in the front. I've never worn it because it's quite revealing. Leave it to Keels to find it in the back of my closet.

"Thank you."

I smile because he's so complimentary but mostly because Charlie has returned carrying a bouquet of red roses. He's wearing one of his bespoke suits. The charcoal gray color accents his blue-grey eyes so well. He's paired it with a white dress shirt and tie that looks like it's got hints of pinks and purples. He looks amazing. I scan down his long legs to his shoes. Black and shiny and no doubt expensive. Damn, he looks good enough to eat.

Oh, crud. I blush thinking about that.

"What?" he asks, looking somewhat confused.

"What?" I say in an attempt to divert suspicion.

"You're blushing."

"Oh, uh, I just think you look very handsome."

"I do? Thank you." He slides his hand over his tie as he approaches me. Setting the flowers on the small dining table, I watch as he moves in close enough to wrap his arms around me. He smells so good. I lean in and sniff at that spot below his ear.

"Sadie?"

"Yeah," I say wistfully.

"Are you smelling me?"

"Yeah. You smell so good." I do something unusual for me. I kiss the spot below his ear. Then, this is the part that's out of character, I swipe my tongue over the same spot. It elicits an amazing sound from him—a combination of a groan and a growl.

"Sadie?" he says huskily.

"Yeah?"

"If you do that again, we'll be late for dinner."

"So?" I remain wrapped in his arms.

"You need to eat."

I pull my head back and smirk. "I do?"

"Sadie," he warns, but he's giving me a sexy-as-sin smile. "I take it you're feeling better?"

"I am. I haven't gotten sick all day." And it's awesome.

Patting my behind, Charlie takes me by the hands. "Food. Then we'll see about your little innuendo."

"Innuendo? Moi?" I say, fluttering my lashes and feigning innocence.

I chose to take Charlie to the best Italian place this side of the

Missouri River, Giovanni's. I get takeout from here often since it's located kitty-corner from my bakery. We're seated near the back of the restaurant, and if I crane my neck, I can just see the sign for Sadie Cakes. The tables are covered in white linens; small votive candles flicker, giving the room a warm glow. The restaurant is painted in deep reds and browns, making the room cozy. It's a popular restaurant, so there are only one or two empty tables.

"What's good here?" Charlie asks as he looks at his menu.

"Everything. They're known for the lasagna. Honestly, you can't go wrong with anything."

When the waiter stops by the table, I recognize him. "Hey, Sadie. How you doin'?"

"Good. How are you, Ryan?"

"Good."

Silence. Ryan is only sixteen and Polly's nephew; he hasn't yet learned the art of the conversation. That's okay; he's a sweet guy and a very hard worker. I've had him help out at the bakery from time to time.

"So, shall we order?" asks Charlie.

I go first and order the lasagna and Caesar side salad. When Charlie looks torn, I say, "Get something different. We can share."

"Wonderful. Thank you, darling."

Oh, he broke out the darling. I love that.

"I'll have the chicken piccata and a Caesar side salad as well."

Once our orders are in, I'm about to ask him about Laura when a shadow falls over our white linens. "Well hello, Sadie."

I look up and see Beryl Winchester dressed to the nines. She's always dressed perfectly, but it's going a little overboard at this place. Don't get me wrong, the restaurant is very nice, but it's not sequined cocktail dress nice. If you know what I mean. I look up to make eye contact. I learned a long time ago to always make eye contact with Beryl Winchester. If you don't, she'll see weakness. I'd like to tell you she is smiling at me, but honestly, I can't be sure about her expressions anymore, thanks to monthly Botox treatments. True story.

"Hello, Beryl." I'd ask what she's doing here in Page but I'm sure it has something to do with her business or her son or maybe it's both. I want to stand up and wrap my fingers around her scrawny neck for tricking me. But I can't worry about that right this minute. I will, though. As soon as I sit down with my sisters, we'll deal with it as a family.

"Good evening, Sadie." She pauses, first looking at me, then at Charlie.

"Beryl, this is Charlie."

Charlie stands to greet her. "Beryl. I believe you know my grandmother."

"Oh? I highly doubt that," she says in a haughty voice.

"Laura? Laura Storrance-Ashbury?"

It's comical to watch the change in expression on her face. Haughty just changed to confused, then to realization. "Well, my goodness," she coos with her hand extended like she expects him to kiss it. "Laura's grandson? It's delightful to meet any relation to Laura." Her voice has taken on a squeaky, high-pitched quality that, frankly, makes me wince.

"How do you know our Sa...?" Her sentence stops suddenly. She looks to me. "Well, well, well, Sadie. You're a clever one, aren't you?"

"Excuse me?" Charlie sits back down slowly.

Turning back to Charlie, Beryl snarls, "Did she tell you," she points at my stomach, "that the baby is yours?"

Charlie slowly nods.

In a diabolical way you only hear in movies, Beryl laughs.

"If I were you, son, I'd make sure of that. She was with my son right up until that cruise. If you know what I mean."

I stare at her with my mouth agape. "Beryl?"

"Yes?"

"How's Candy?" Yes, I know how catty that is. But, in my defense, she's a sneaky snake. Catty is definitely called for when it comes to her.

Her face morphs again from snooty to fake and smiling. "She's a peach."

A peach? "And her children?"

"Delightful. Like my own grandchildren."

Wow. I know she's lying, but why? "Great. Glad to hear it. I hope you'll all be happy."

CHAPTER TWENTY-THREE

SADIE

WHEN RYAN APPROACHES our table with our salads, I thank the food service gods for the interruption.

"Well, I'll leave you to it." She turns to go. "Oh, and Sadie?"

"Yeah?" I look up at her.

"I'll be in touch about the bakery."

My fork stops midair on its way down to pierce a fresh leafy green. Instead of stabbing the lettuce, I set the silverware back down. "What about the bakery?"

"I believe it's time for some changes."

"What kind of changes?" I'm biting the inside of my mouth to keep from screaming at the top of my lungs.

"Oh, nothing to worry your pretty little head about tonight. Just some issues with mismanagement."

"Mismanagement?" *I'm* the management.

Beryl turns to Charlie. "It was lovely to meet you. Best to your family, Charles."

But not best to mine? She never liked my sisters or my father. That should have been my first indication to hightail it as far away from Andrew as I could.

Charlie nods and smiles at Beryl. It looks sincere, but how can it be? He knows what she's doing to me.

"Charlie? Did you hear what she said?"

Distracted, he picks up his fork.

"I did."

"And?"

"She wants to meet. You should meet."

Is he serious right now? "Well, gee. Thanks for that piece of legal advice."

"I merely played your attorney, Sadie. I'm not actually your lawyer."

"Right."

"But you should probably get one."

"Right." I stab my lettuce with a vengeance, knowing full well it doesn't deserve it. "Thanks."

We eat our salad in silence. When our entrees are served, I slide my plate into the middle of the table and grab a forkful of lasagna. As I bring the utensil to my mouth, I peek up at Charlie, expecting him to dig into the cheesy goodness, but that's not what I see. There's a crease between his brows. Does this bother him? "What?"

"Why don't I cut a portion of the lasagna away and set it on my plate? Then you can eat with your plate in front of you?" He has a smile on his face, but I know passive-aggressive when I see it. I wrote the goddamn book on passive-aggressive.

"You know what?" I set my napkin on the table. "I'm not feeling great."

"Oh?" He starts to stand. "Are you going to be ill?" His face a mix of concern and something else.

"No. Sit. I'll just go powder my nose until it passes." I stand from the table. "I'll be back." *Eventually.*

I take my purse with me and make my way to the hallway that leads to the bathroom. I'm not actually feeling unwell. I just need a break to process what happened back there. Charlie's entire face changed the minute Beryl suggested Andrew could be the father. I could reassure him by telling him that there's no way Andrew could be the father because 1) I was on birth control the last time Andrew and I had sex, 2) He used a condom on top of that, and 3) It was a solid month prior to the cruise that we'd had any sort of action, and I think it was merely a hand job one morning. So, there's no way Andrew is the father, but an ultrasound should reassure him. It'll give him proof of the timeline. I can't blame Charlie, really. If the situation were reversed, wouldn't I want to be sure? Damn straight. He just took my word for it. Word from a woman he barely knows. I need to cut Charlie some slack. This—I run my palm over my stomach—is a life-changing event. We need to be sure we're doing everything right. When it's safe for the baby, we'll get a paternity test.

When I exit the restroom, I nearly run into the head chef for the restaurant. I've done some pastry work for her before. I wave hello. "Delicious tonight, Chef."

"Thank you, Sadie," Antonia says in a thick Italian accent. She's legit Italian. From Italy. I think that's what makes her food so good. I snort to myself as I walk down the hallway. On the way to the table, I look left and get a glimpse of my bakery across the street. I halt when I see a light on at the shop. Light glowing from the back of the store. Checking the time, I frown. "Polly had better not be working late."

I look over and see Charlie doing something on his phone, so I decide to check out my store before returning to the table. He won't even know I'm gone. I'll only be a minute. I quickly jog across the street and peek through the glass door. I'm about to use my key when I notice the door is open. Polly wouldn't do that. She's careful about her safety. Pushing it open a few inches, I lean my head in to listen and I immediately hear voices. More than one. And laughter. Children's laughter. "What the fuck?" I whisper.

Stepping back with my back against the solid brick wall, I pull my phone out and dial 9-1-1.

"Nine-one-one, what is your emergency?"

In a husky whisper, I say, "Someone has broken into my business. The door was ajar. I hear voices from the back room."

"We'll dispatch someone right away. What's the address?"

I give the address as she asks, "Are you in the store, ma'am?"

"No. I'm outside."

"Stay there. We have a patrol in the area."

"Right." I'm about to do just that when I crane my neck enough to see into the glass door again. It's then I see someone come into the front of the shop from the back. A child. One I've seen from time to time. Candy's oldest. "What the ever-loving hell?"

Ignoring the advice of the Page P.D. dispatcher, I step through the front door and straight through to the back. When I see what's happening, I'm struck dumb. "What the fuck is going on here?" I yell at the top of my lungs.

I've definitely caught their attention. All of them. Andrew, Candy, and Candy's youngest are all in the back of my shop, standing around my stainless steel table. "Andrew? I asked you a question."

"What's it look like? We're having dessert." His expression is smug. Not to mention he's got white buttercream icing all over his chin. Idiot.

I hear Candy giggle as she bites into a piece of cake. And not just any cake. A wedding cake. A wedding cake that I made and decorated for the Carmichael-McCallister wedding. They're eating a fucking bakery order that is supposed to go out tomorrow and one that cost me a fuck-ton of money and time to make. I'm seething. I've never wanted to kill someone more in my life. Not even that time Agatha cut the hair on all my Barbies to look like Drew Barrymore in her pixie haircut stage.

"Why did you have to ruin all five tiers of cake?" Jesus. They cut hunks out of each layer.

Andrew just shrugs. "We thought they would be different flavors, but they were all lemon. Who does that?"

"Everyone." Well, not everyone, but lots of people. "How did you get in here?"

"I have a key. I own the building, remember?"

"Andy, honey?" squeaks Candy. "Anvil needs to use the potty."

Anvil? I don't think I knew the poor kid's name. She always calls her kids rude things rather than their actual names.

Andrew nods. "Back there." He nods to my one and only restroom. "You know," he continues as he wipes his face off with one of my clean aprons. "You surprised me."

"How so?" You prick.

"How so? Well, I had no idea you were such a money-grubbing whore."

"A-A what?" *A whore?* How dare he?

"You didn't wait five minutes before jumping on the first rich dick in sight, did you?"

"Andrew!" I shout because damn, he's pissing me off. "That's not—"

I'm about to launch into a rant to end all rants when two policemen step through the swinging doors, guns drawn. "Freeze!" yells the oldest guy on the force, and a friend of my dad's, Sergeant Malcolm Baker.

"Good evening, officers," Andrew says, being smarmy and gross.

Candy steps through the door and around the officers, children in tow, until she's next to Andrew.

I point to the four of them, even the kids, while I address Malcolm and our newest cop here in Page. "They broke in and are eating Dan McCallister's wedding cake." Dan's a cop. They'll understand.

"You're eating Dan's cake?" says an officer I've only met one other time, Nick Martelli.

Andrew shrugs. I watch as the other of Candy's precious angels reaches up and grabs a glob of cake from the only side of the cake that hadn't been destroyed.

"Shit," mutters Malcolm. "I'd better let Dan know." He steps toward the swinging doors on the way out of the room.

Great. Now Dan is going to hate me, and he'll never stop by for coffee and his lemon blueberry cupcakes. "Wait! Malcolm." He stops walking. "Tell him I'll make another one, if I have to stay up all night."

"Will do, sweetie."

Turning back to Officer Martelli, I say, "Andrew owns the building. Apparently, he thinks he has the right to come in here and treat himself to whatever he wants."

"I'm a silent partner too." He turns to look at me, his eyes angry slits, "I know you know. Lance called me today."

Ignoring the asshole, I turn to Officer Martelli. "That's not the issue here. You've essentially stolen from me. You've destroyed property." I look over at Nick pleadingly. "Right?"

"Nah, I don't think the cops see it that way, do you, officer?" Andrew says like the cocky asshole he is.

I look over at Nick, hoping and praying he's going to help me out.

"Sadie, this seems like a legal matter. But we'll file a report. Destruction of property seems plausible."

Not so much. *Thanks for nothing, Nick.*

Nick pulls out a notebook from his breast pocket. "Sir? Can I get your name?"

"Andrew Winchester." His chest puffs out like a rooster as he says his name. "I'm sure you've heard of me."

"Not really, no, sir. And you, ma'am?" he nods to Candy.

"Candy P. Cane, Mr. Officer."

Mr. Officer? Jesus.

"What's the *P* stand for, Ms. Cane?"

I swear to all that's holy, if she says Peppermint, I'm going to lose it.

"Prudence."

I snort. I can't help it. *Prudence?* What the hell?

Ignoring my small outburst, Nick turns to Andrew. "I'd advise you to leave the premises, sir, ma'am," he says, looking at Candy.

"Fine." Andrew says, sounding defeated, but I know him. He's just playing the part. Turning back to me, he says with a stupid wink, "I'll be in touch, Sadie."

Candy is staring at Nick like he's dessert rather than law enforcement. Not surprising—Nick Martelli is *not* ugly. Far from it. If there were a Hot Cops of the Month calendar, Nick Martelli would be Mr. June, July, *and* August. He's that hot.

"Of course, officer," Candy says in that high-pitched voice of hers that grates on my last fucking nerve. She steps closer to him.

I swear she's reaching for his chest when Nick backs up. "Ma'am? Step back."

"Oh, pooh," she simpers, "I wasn't going to hurt you." God, she sounds just like Marilyn Monroe in the movie *The Seven Year Itch.* (No offense to the late, great Ms. Monroe.)

I'm about to interrupt their little tête-à-tête when the door swings open, revealing Charlie. An angry-looking Charlie. That's a look I've never seen before and I'm not sure I like it. "What the hell is going on here?"

"Charlie, I—"

He looks at me. "You just left me at the table?" Running a hand through his hair, he continues, "I saw the police lights and watched them run in here with their guns drawn." He strides toward me and wraps an arm around me. "Jesus, I thought you'd been shot, Sadie."

"Shot, no. Screwed over, yes," I mumble to myself.

Officer Nick interrupts us by reminding Andrew and his crew it's time to leave and not to return until everything has been sorted legally.

"B-but—" Andrew starts to say.

"You heard me, Mr. Winchester." Wow, Nick Martelli is sort of hot when he's bossy. I've heard that about him, actually.

"Fine."

"What about the wedding cake? I'm out several hundred dollars."

"For that?" Andrew spits out. "It was average, at best. Who'd request a lemon cake for a wedding?"

"Dan McCallister and Meghan Carmichael. That's who," I deadpan.

I watch as Andrew walks out the door, leaving Candy and her children behind. Candy's too busy staring at Nick to realize he's gone.

"He's leaving," I snap.

"Oh," she giggles. "Let's go, you little shits." See? Told you. She holds one hand of each child, hands still covered in cake and frosting, by the way, and walks out of the room. I can't help noticing her outfit. She's wearing a white tank top, no bra, gray sweat pants that she cut off so short you can see her ass cheeks, and red stilettos. Classy.

I'm thinking Officer Martelli isn't impressed with the endearments she's given her kids either. At least the scowl he just gave her says he isn't. Looking back at me, he returns to professional mode. "Let me write this up, Sadie. Be right back. I'll need you to sign it." Before he exits the bakery, he says, "Oh, and I'd take pictures of this mess if I were you. Out here too." He points to the front of my store.

"Great. What'd they do out there?"

"You probably don't want to know."

I nod, staring at what remains of my five-tiered masterpiece. "While you do that, I'm going to call Meghan and Dan. I want them to know I'm going to make a new cake in time for the wedding."

I walk to the back of the room to make the call in my office. I'm glad I did. Meghan is sobbing on the other end of the line. When I feel as though she's gotten her emotions under control, I walk out of my office, to the back of the shop, grab the large-wheeled garbage can and roll it over to the work table. I hear clicking noises and see Charlie taking photos of the mess. When he's done, I use one hand to sweep the largest layer into the trash can first. Then the four other layers after that. Next, I grab the disinfectant from the sink area and clean the table thoroughly.

With the table clean, I begin to gather up my ingredients.

"What are you doing?"

"Huh?" I look up to see Charlie with hands on his hips.

"I asked you what you were doing."

"What's it look like?" *Duh.* "I'm making a wedding cake."

"They ate a wedding cake?" Charlie walked into the scene late, so he missed that part.

"Yep. When I asked Andrew what he was doing?" I pause for effect. "He said they were 'having dessert.'"

"Dessert? He ate a wedding cake that didn't belong to him for dessert?" Charlie's running his palms through his hair. "What is wrong with these people?"

I chuckle, but not because it's funny. "They're terrible people. Terrible people who are going to take away my dream, mine and my mom's, to own a little bakery." I feel the burn of tears, but I won't cry. I'll deal with whatever they throw at me. This isn't the worst thing that has happened to me in my life. My mom dying was the worst. I'd give up a trillion bakeries to have her back for just one day.

So, yeah, I can do something else for a while. I could work for a restaurant or two around town. I could drive down to Flagstaff and do catering like Aggie. Then maybe I'd start over in a few years. The baby will be here in no time. I could live with Violet or my dad and be very happy.

Shit. Here they come. One tear after another starts to slide out of my eyes and down my cheeks.

I sense him before I feel him. Wrapping his strong arms around me, he leans in to whisper, "I'm sorry, sweetheart."

I nod and sniffle. I can't bring myself to speak.

"What can I do to help?" Charlie says softly while still holding me.

Where do I start?

I turn my head and watch him as he removes his jacket and starts to roll up his sleeves. "Got an apron?"

"You know how to bake?"

"No. But I can follow directions. I can prep baking pans, things of that nature."

I laugh through a tear or two. I can't help it. This guy is something. "Good. Aprons are in that drawer over there." I point to a large cabinet in the corner. "Get me one?"

"Sure thing, beautiful."

With everything out, I explain the process. "Luckily, I have extra cake made for the base layer. I always do that, just in case. I'll need to bake the remaining layers and get them into the blast freezer."

"You freeze the cake?"

"It's easier to ice and decorate if it's frozen. You don't get crumbs in the icing."

"The dreaded crumbs," he mumbles as he covers the inside of each layer pan with oil.

"Indeed."

We work in companionable silence for a good long while. That is, until he asks. "Sadie?"

I know what's coming.

With a deep breath, I say what I wanted to say at the restaurant. "I know what you're going to say, and, Charlie, the baby is yours, but I'll understand if you need a paternity test. I would." I shrug. "But you should know Andrew and I hadn't been, er, intimate enough to make a baby for over a month before the cruise. So the ultrasound will tell you everything you need to know. If you still feel unsure, let's find out when we can have a paternity test done safely." I said that entire thing without looking up at him. It hurt to say it. I wish he just believed me.

"Sadie. That's not what I was going to say. I believe you. Even though we're only just getting to know one another, I feel like you're the realest person I've ever met."

"Okay. If that wasn't the question, what was it?"

"I wanted to apologize for what I said about getting an attorney. That was rude. But I was taken aback by Beryl Winchester. I've met some ruthless people in my life, but I think Beryl may take the cake." He smirks. "No pun intended."

"None taken," I deadpan.

"To think she duped you like that while you were practically engaged to that ass of a son of hers."

"I know."

"So, if you need an attorney, I'd be happy to do what I can to help you, but I'm a bit rusty. I do have a friend here in Arizona who would be a good fit for this situation."

"We'll see." Now I look up at him. "By the way, I feel that way about you too even though you're rich as Croesus."

"Gee, thanks, honey." He chuckles as he sets the last pan down. "Now what?"

"Wanna learn how to make buttercream icing? It's super fun!" I lift my brows up and down to get him excited.

"Sure. Why not?"

I give him the recipe and we work together to make the most delicious icing known to man. I could eat it with a spoon if it wouldn't launch me into a sugar coma.

CHAPTER TWENTY-FOUR

Charlie

"LAURA WILL BE HERE TOMORROW."

"Oh?" she asks absently. She's taking lemon cake from the layer pans I helped prepare. I feel a sense of pride knowing I was part of this process.

"She's in Sedona already. She'll drive up to the house and be here by midafternoon. She wants us to meet her there."

"Okay." Sadie starts to lift a large tray that holds multiple layers of cake. I race to her side and attempt to take the pan. It looks heavy.

"No," she snaps, "I've got it."

"It looks heavy." I think I just whined. A little bit.

"It is. But I've done this for years and years. I've got the upper body strength."

"Fine." I'm not happy about it. I'm about to tell her that she'll have to stop doing that in a month or two but think better of it. We're having a good time. I'm learning how to bake. It's relaxing, for the most part. I can see why she does it.

"What happens next?"

"I'll put this in the blast freezer while I start to ice the bottom layer I've got in the walk-in freezer."

This time, she allows me to carry the large bottom layers to the table.

"Pull up a chair. I'll explain what I'm doing as I decorate."

Finding two stools off in the corner, I bring us each one. "Not for me. I need to stand for this."

I watch in amazement as Sadie ices each layer of the wedding cake. Her hands move lightning fast, the cream sliding perfectly into place. She makes it look easy, but I suspect it's not. Next, she places each layer onto a spinning plate contraption and begins to decorate. "Luckily, most of this cake will have fresh flowers all around it. I only need to pipe shells on the edges and add Cornelli lace to layers two and four."

"What about one, three, and five?"

"Ah, well, three and five will be basket weave, and the top layer will be decorated with polka dots."

Setting to work on the top layer, Sadie's got polka dots covering it in no time. Placing that on a pan, she slides it onto a baking rack. Next, she works on the Cornelli lace layers. Layers one, two, and four are finished in record time. It's the basket weave on layers three and five that takes time.

But Sadie reassures me, "I've done it so many times; it doesn't take as long as you'd think."

Just as she starts layer three, my phone vibrates.

"Well, that's weird." I mumble to myself. It's nearly three in the morning and I'm getting phone calls? When I peer down at the name on the screen, I stand up. "I need to take this." I nod toward the door. "Back in a minute."

I step out of the bakery to take a call from the General

Manager of the Los Angeles Diamonds. I know what this call means. I'm needed elsewhere. Now, I'll have to figure out how to break the news to Sadie. Stepping back into the kitchen, I give Sadie a smile.

"Good news?" she asks when I return.

"Not necessarily. Why do you ask?"

"You have a big smile on your face."

"I'm just happy to see you," I say, surprised at my own words. But it's the truth.

"Aw, that's sweet. Wanna watch me do this layer of basket weave? It's cool."

"Sure."

"You know? You haven't even asked to try a cupcake. Usually the minute people walk in they want a treat. You're not into sweets?"

"I love them. I just didn't want you to think I was after you for your cake."

That makes her laugh. "I don't mind you wanting me for my cake, Charlie. It's part of me."

With a fake sigh, I turn toward the front of the store. "If you insist. I did spot one or two out there that would make my year."

"Go get 'em. And bring me one."

"Which one?"

"Surprise me."

Selecting three cupcakes, I return to Sadie.

"I'm rather curious to know what you picked for me and for yourself?"

"Why is that?"

"It says a lot about a person."

"All right. Tell me who I am." I place a Raspberry Ripple cupcake in front of Sadie. "I chose a Raspberry Ripple for you. And before you ask, it's because it's pink and soft, like your lips."

"Oh, you're good."

I watch as a blush rushes to her cheeks.

"What'd you pick for yourself?"

"A white cupcake with white icing."

"Interesting. You're traditional."

"I am fairly traditional but to mix it up, I picked the Mexican Hot Chocolate cupcake."

"Ooh, a little risk to go along with your traditional side?"

"Exactly."

She stares at me as I bite into the chocolate cupcake.

"I love to see the expressions on people's faces when they eat my treats. This one has some spice to it."

As soon as I bite down, my eyes squeeze shut, and a sound that hopefully tells her how delicious her cake is rumbles from deep in my chest.

"I love to hear that sound." Her eyes haven't left my face.

I finish the cupcake in two more bites. "Wow. That was amazing, Sadie." I smile and can tell I've got bits of chocolate in my teeth. I lick my lips and go right for the vanilla cupcake. Damn, it's almost as good as the first one. Almost. "Both were amazing, but I think I prefer the chocolate. It was unexpected—something outside the box." I smile at Sadie. "And I'm starting to like the unexpected."

"I'm glad. Feel free to try other flavors."

"I'll try them all eventually. I've got plenty of time. I could be your permanent taste tester."

Sadie giggles. "Good to know."

Finishing up layer three, she rotates the cake to show me. "What do you think?"

I stand and walk to her until I'm at her back. Wrapping my arms around her waist again, I lean down and kiss her neck. "I think," I kiss the same spot, "you're amazing." This time I nibble on her neck and feel her skin pebble. "You taste so sweet," I say in a husky voice.

"You'd better stop that. I only have one more layer. Then we can go home."

"Home. I like the sound of that. I'll especially like it when it really is our home and not a hotel room."

"Mm-hm," she mumbles. "Fifteen more minutes."

I'm surprised she didn't jump on that statement. I'll leave it there. For now.

I continue to watch as she turns lemon cake batter and white frosting into something beautiful. When I look at my watch, I realize we've been here for hours. Once she's finished, I help her roll a metal cart filled with the layers into the cooler.

Stepping out the back door, I wait as she locks the door behind us. "You need a security system."

"Beryl will require the code. It's their building, as they keep reminding me." She sighs sadly. "I'll just have to accept the fact that they're going to do what they need to do and that's either shut me down or take over. I can't afford an attorney." She turns and points her finger at me. "And I'm not taking a cent from you."

I shrug, but inside I'm irritated. Why won't she take my money? "Fine." No worries. I have my ways of helping Sadie without using my money.

"There's one more thing."

She makes a grumbling sound as we make our way to my car. "What?"

"I'm leaving day after tomorrow."

She stops moving. "Okay."

Okay? Just okay? "Don't you want to know where I'm going?"

"I assume you're going home."

"No, I'm not going to Boston." At the car, I move to stand in front of her. I need to see her eyes. They give away everything she's thinking.

"I'm going to Los Angeles for an ACL surgery on an NBA player." With my hand on her wrist, I tug her toward me until she's facing me. "Then I'll be back. I usually stick around a few days after surgery for post-op care." The stubborn woman hasn't made eye contact with me yet. "Sadie?"

"What?"

She's looking at my left ear, and it's making me crazy. "Look at me. Please." When she finally looks me in the eye, I say, "I'll be back. This is how my job works. I fly out for a few days, then I fly back."

"Sure. I get that."

"But?" There's a but in there.

"But for how long? Are you going to hang out until the baby's born and then go home? Because, at this point, I won't be leaving Page anytime soon. Unless Beryl and Andrew get their wish. Then I'd have all the time in the world. Still, I don't want to leave my family. They're too important to me. Besides, I want them to be a part of Peanut's life." Sadie looks into my eyes this time. Finally. And she's *really* looking. "That's not fair to *your* family, though, is it?"

I shrug. "My family is different. They can jump on one of Laura's planes and visit, or we can jump on Laura's plane and visit them."

"God, you make it sound so easy." She chuckles. "She has more than one plane?"

I nod. "Why does it have to be difficult? People have children all the time. Lots of families live in different states. We're not unique."

"So, you're willing to stay here," she points at the floor, "in Page, Arizona?"

"More than willing. I hired a realtor today to find us a house."

She starts to pull back from me in an attempt to escape my arms. "You bought a house? For us? *Us?*"

"I haven't yet. I'd never buy a home without you approving of it."

Turning away from me, Sadie begins to pace. "We barely know each other and you're going to buy a house. For *us?*"

"We'll get to know each other."

Her pacing is now in double time. "Shit, Charlie. Knowing you, you'll buy some mega-mansion out on Rainbow Road. A mega-mansion with a mortgage I won't be able to afford to pay half of."

"No. You don't—"

Halting, she faces me. "Do *not* tell me I don't have to pay."

"Sadie. We'll house hunt together. We'll find something that's affordable for me *and* you. Something big enough for Peanut to have room to play."

"Oh." She stops pacing and places a palm over her abdomen. "Peanut will need room to play, won't she?"

"She?"

"Or he," she corrects quickly. "Either one, as long as they've got ten fingers and ten toes, as they say."

I take three steps to get to her and wrap her in my arms again. "As long as Peanut is healthy." I lean down and kiss her softly. "Speaking of which, let's get home. I'm ready to get you into bed."

"Oh, Charlie. I'm too tired—"

"To sleep. We both need sleep."

"That we do."

~

WE FINALLY DRAG our asses back to the hotel at three in the morning. That experience was exhausting, and I wasn't even doing much of the work. After we finished, Sadie left Polly a lengthy note about the cake debacle. She also sent her a text relaying the same information so she could sleep in without worrying about any of it. I'm glad she's taking another day off. She needs it after spending most of the evening and night at the bakery.

Which reminds me. "We never got to finish our dinners."

"No, we didn't." Sadie has stripped out of her dress and into a Sadie Cakes tee in minutes. I watch her pull the bedding down and slide in. "I'll stop in there tomorrow and pay the bill."

"No worries, I paid the bill. I was looking forward to eating that food, though."

"Tomorrow night?" she asks tentatively. "We could get takeout and watch a movie."

"Laura will be in town. I'm sure she'll want to dine with us."

"Dine with us," Sadie says, half to herself. "I may never get used to the way you talk, Charlie."

"What's wrong with the way I talk?" I'm unbuttoning my dress shirt as I ask.

With a yawn she says, "Hoity toity."

"I take offense to that, Sadie." I really do. I pause before I unbuckle my belt and slacks. "Just because my vocabulary is different doesn't mean something is wrong with the way I speak."

She rolls over to look at me. "You take offense?" Pushing herself up onto her elbows, she furrows her brow. "I'm sorry. I didn't mean it like that. I like the way you speak. Especially the way you talk to me. I was teasing."

Kicking away my pants, I slide into bed in only my boxer briefs. "Good. Because I can't very well change that."

"Charlie?" she asks, sounding sincerely worried. "I'd never ask you to change."

Rolling to face her, I slide my palm up her bare arm. "Good. I'll never ask you to change either." Leaning in, I kiss her lips, then the tip of her nose. "I'm beat. Let's sleep."

"Agreed."

Reaching back, I snap off the light beside my bed, darkening the room immediately.

"I wish I had a fan," Sadie says aloud. "I sleep better with white noise."

"Noted. I'll get you a fan tomorrow, my sweet." I kiss the top of her head.

"Aw. You say the cutest things to me."

"Now I say cute things. Hm, I'm sort of complex, aren't I?"

Giggling, she slides close enough to place her head on my shoulder. "You're super complex, Mr. Assberry. It's hot."

"Complex and hot." I pull her in closer until she's snuggled right up against me. "I'll take it."

CHAPTER TWENTY-FIVE

SADIE

I CAN'T SLEEP. It could be due to the adrenaline from making a wedding cake at the last minute. I could be nervous about Laura's visit tomorrow, or that Charlie is going to buy a house for *us*. Or maybe it's because he's leaving. I know it's only for a few days but yeah, I think that's the part that's troubling me the most. I've become attached to the man lying beside me. In just a few days, I've bonded with him in a way I never did with Andrew.

It's not surprising I feel more connected to Charlie than Andrew. I mean, Andrew and Charlie are two completely different men. Sure, they both come from money and grew up in that lifestyle, but as people? As real men? There's no comparison. Perhaps I should thank Andrew. Thank him for sleeping with Candy P. Cane in my bed. Because if I hadn't caught the two of them, I'd probably be engaged to him right now and I may even be pregnant with *his* baby. There's no question which of the two men I'd want to be the father of my child. Just imagine Andrew as a father. His entire life has always been about him. That means Peanut's life would be second to his—in his mind.

I may be projecting some of my hostility on the man but deep down, I know I dodged a damn bullet there.

"Thank goodness," I whisper to myself.

"Thank goodness for what?" says a sleepy Charlie as his arms wrap around my middle, pulling me closer to him.

"Shh, go back to sleep. I was just talking to myself."

I feel his lips touch my bare shoulder, then slowly move up my neck. Like soft butterfly kisses all the way to my mouth. When they reach my lips, those kisses change from soft to much more urgent. I feel him harden against my leg. I'm not going to lie; the man turns me on with a mere touch. Couple that with the way he just sort of rolled me onto my back and slid himself between my legs until he had me pressed against him—that move alone is making me crazy aroused. God, I want him.

Charlie breaks away from the kiss, all the while pushing my Sadie Cakes Bakery tee up my torso, urging it up and off. I help by raising my arms. All that's left are my practical cotton Hanes Her Way undies. *At least they're pink.* But those only last a minute more before they're tossed away somewhere into the dark room.

I make an attempt to move up to him, but he uses his palm to press me back down. His hands slide down to cup my breasts, each of his fingers playing with my sensitive nipples like he's a maestro and I'm his instrument. I writhe and moan at his touch. "Charlie," I say in a husky voice.

"Shh, beautiful. Let me please you."

Let me please you? Oh, yes. Yes. Yes. Yes.

His mouth first licks, then suckles on each breast. "Charlie," I whine.

Ignoring me, Charlie's mouth moves down. He spends extra time kissing my stomach, right where Peanut resides. It's so sweet. If I weren't ready to pop like a July Fourth firecracker, I'd say so. His warm hands slide down to my knees, then inward until he's pressing my legs open wider. Oh, God. Is he...?

He is. His mouth is over my—my area down there, his tongue flicking in and out, pressing into me while his lips kiss and suck the most sensitive parts of me. I don't ever remember my clitoris being this happy before. Well, maybe the other times I've been with Charlie. She's been pretty happy those times too.

Reaching down, I run my fingers through his wavy hair. Grasping a chunk, I press him into me. I can't help it. He's making me do it. "Don't stop. Please, baby," I say breathlessly.

But he does. That bastard stops.

"You called me baby."

I'm blinking furiously because I can't believe he stopped. For that. "Yeah?" And?

"I liked it." He swipes his tongue through me, and I moan. "I liked it a lot. My cock is harder than granite after that."

"Okay." Pulling his hair not so gently, I do what I have to do to get him back to work. "Please, Charlie."

He stops again and in the deepest, growliest voice I've ever heard, he says, "Baby. When I'm doing this, when my tongue is inside you, when I'm fucking you—you call me baby."

"Fine. Please, baby. Don't stop."

"Tell me to lick this pussy."

"Lick me." I pant.

"Say it."

Oh, God. This uptight fancy man is so dirty. "Pl-please, lick my pussy." I add, "Baby" for good measure. And it works, because Charlie goes caveman on me.

"Fuck. You taste so fucking delicious, Sadie."

He nibbles on my outer lips and pinches my clitoris, and

that's all it takes. I lose it. I come like a cannon. But Charlie's not done. "One more. I want one more from you." With his hands on my hips, he urges me up onto my knees. I'm exhausted but I comply. Charlie rolls onto his back, all the while urging me closer. "Straddle my face."

"Charlie?" That is not going to be a good look for me.

"Now."

Oh, he broke out the boss again. So I do it. I bring my leg over him and scoot up closer to his mouth. "You're so bossy."

"You like it. Don't you, my good girl?"

"Oh, fuck yes." I swear that almost made me come again.

"Lower yourself."

Holding on to the headboard, I lower myself. I'm going to crush him, suffocate him. I know it. How will I explain that to his family? Laura will hate me. Shit, my sisters. Keely will never let me live it down. When his tongue starts to work on me again, I abandon all of my worries. "Fuck it," I mutter. This feels too good to stop.

"You want me to fuck you?"

"Eventually. Don't stop."

But he does.

"Baby." I remembered. "Baby, please don't stop."

"That's my girl."

It takes short work for me to come again. I need to move off him, but he's still holding me in place, licking slowly. It's like he's savoring me. And to think Andrew never wanted to do this. To me, anyway. Candy P. Cane was another story.

Moving my leg back over, I kneel next to him. Peering down at his, his... okay, I'll say it. His cock. It's practically vibrating. It's moving and twitching like it's trying to get closer to me. I guess turnabout is fair play. I haven't gone down on him yet. Leaning over him, I look up into his eyes to gauge his reaction. He nods quickly. "Either suck me or ride me, honey. Your pick."

"Both."

"Sweet mother...," he moans as I swipe my tongue over the tip. "You're amazing. So fucking beautiful." His reaction is all I need to propel me onward. I wouldn't say I'm especially proficient at blow jobs, but he makes me want to be better. Placing my mouth on the tip, I suck gently, all the while using my hand to stroke him up and down.

"Fuck. You're killing me." His hips are jutting off the bed in time with my movements. "Suck me. Suck me hard, Sadie."

This man. Such a dirty mouth in bed. And so reserved and polite the rest of the time. I sort of like the fact that I get to see this unbridled side of him while the world only gets fancy Charlie. So I suck harder. And faster.

"If you want me to fuck you, you'd better stop, honey."

And I do. I do want him to fuck me. Sliding him out of my mouth, I lick the tip one last time. "Was that okay?" I ask self-consciously. It sure sounded like he approved, but who knows.

He sits up and I watch his abs flex. "Never better."

I stare at his chest. His body is a work of art. There's a smattering of dark hair that leads down from his pectorals to a line that leads to his cock. His cock that's rigid and glistening from my mouth. I reach out and run my fingers through the hair on his chest, skimming over one of his flat, dark nipples. A shiver runs through him when I do it, so I repeat it over his other one. He's quiet as I touch him. Running both palms over his chest, I pinch his nipples, which elicits a moan from him.

"You're sensitive here too."

"Mm-hmm."

My hands roam over his shoulders, down his strong arms, to his hands, where I touch each finger with my own. These hands, a surgeon's hands, are big and warm; his fingers are long and elegant. I can't help myself. "I hope Peanut gets your hands."

"Why?"

"Because. They're capable. They heal."

Looking at his face, I watch him swallow. His Adam's apple bobs. "Is there anything else you'd like Peanut to get from me?"

I smile at his question. "Your brain, but we already covered that."

Charlie rolls his eyes, so I continue, "I don't know you all that well, Charlie, but from what I can tell so far"—I place my hand over the center of his chest—"you're good, kind, and caring. There's no greater gift you could give our Peanut."

Reaching out, Charlie moves my hair away from my face. I'm betting my hair resembles a wild animal at this point in our sexy time. "That is one of the nicest things anyone has ever said to me."

"I find that hard to believe, Mr. Ashbury."

"Not Assberry?" He chuckles.

"Not when we're talking about Peanut. Her last name will be Ashbury. I can't make fun of it then."

"There you go with 'her' again. Are you telling me you sense a girl in here?" he says as he places his warm palm over my stomach. It stays there, rubbing back and forth over the spot.

"No. Probably just habit. Four sisters, remember?"

"Oh, I remember." His palm moves up until he's cupping one of my breasts.

"Mm." I moan, because damn, they're sensitive.

Gently, Charlie pushes me onto my back, pressing himself between my legs. I feel his fingers move down through my center. "Still wet, I see."

"Always with you." I whisper it so softly there's no way he heard me.

Placing himself at my entrance, he kisses me softly as he slowly presses inside. I half expect him to pull out and thrust in quickly, but that's not what he does. No, this time he kisses my lips, my cheek, my eyelid, my forehead, my ear, and my neck.

All the while moving slowly in and out of me. It's like he's making love to me instead of fucking me. If that makes any sense. The build is slow but steady. His hands are touching me everywhere, like he just likes the feel of my skin, or maybe he's memorizing me. I can't be sure because my mind is on the spot that he keeps touching inside me. "Baby," I gasp.

"Feel good, my sweet girl?"

How does he do that? He knows just the right words to use. I feel so close to him right now. Like he's perfect for me. Like he's my person.

No! I thought that was Andrew before; I don't want to make that mistake again. This is just sex. Really, really good sex.

Wrapping my arms around him, I pull him to me so we're chest to chest. "Yes, Charlie," I whisper in his ear. Then I kiss his neck. "Charlie, I lo—" I don't know what I was going to say. Well, maybe I do, but it's gone the minute I orgasm. Those words are gone, replaced by euphoria. My body is charged with electricity. Every hair on my body is standing on end. The orgasm is so intense, so powerful, I'm shaking from it.

"I know, baby. Me too."

Me too? What does that mean?

I want to ask, but then Charlie stiffens as he presses himself into me, deeper than ever. He's twitching inside me while I squeeze around him tightly. I could get used to orgasms like that, made so much better when we're linked together. I could get used to a lot of things with Charlie Ashbury.

CHAPTER TWENTY-SIX

Charlie

WHEN SADIE and I pull into Laura's driveway, there are three large SUVs parked there. That means only one thing. We haven't even made it to the front door when it pops open, revealing my mother, Emily Ashbury. I take Sadie's hand and lead her up the marble steps.

"Mother? What are you doing here?" It's not like I'm not happy to see her; I just wish I'd been warned. *Laura.*

"Charles," she says as I kiss both of her cheeks.

"You remember Sadie?"

"We knew you as Rachel but yes, I remember you. How could I forget?"

Stepping into the foyer of Laura's home, I can't help but feel a sense of foreboding. I didn't miss the fact that she didn't respond to my question, so I repeat it. "What are you doing here?"

"Your grandmother insisted we all fly with her to this

godforsaken place. She said you had an announcement to make."

"You *all*?"

"Yes. All."

I'm holding Sadie's hand, so I can feel it become clammy. Leaning down, I kiss the top of her head. "No worries."

"Uh-huh," she mumbles. "Right."

Stepping into the large living area with floor-to-ceiling windows that overlook a breathtaking view of a large lake, I smile at the feel of the space. The room is comfortable in warm hues of brown, beige, and maroon. There isn't one pretentious thing about the space. It's all Laura.

"Good afternoon, everyone."

My family mumbles their salutations. Scanning the room, I see my father; Cortland; Catherine; her fiancé, Clayton; and Victoria.

Why the hell is Victoria here?

Each person has found a portion of the room to call their own. My father is in an overstuffed chair reading the *Wall Street Journal*. Cortland is playing on his phone, as usual. Catherine is quietly reading as Clayton stares out the window. And then there's Victoria. She's dressed for something more formal in a black dress that is too short and too low cut for this little family get-together.

I grip Sadie's hand harder than I probably need to because, for some reason, I feel a bit untethered. I ask, "Where's Laura?" She's the only person who can make this situation less tumultuous.

"Right here, darling."

Sadie and I turn to see my grandmother, wearing a floral sundress, sweep into the room like she owns the place. Well, she does own the place, so....

"Laura," Sadie says as a gust of wind leaves her. Nerves. I

recognize the reaction. Seeing Laura gives her a sense of relief. For now, anyway. I squeeze her hand gently in the hopes I can give her reassurance.

"Sadie, my dear." Laura pulls Sadie into her arms and squeezes her tightly. "So wonderful to see you again. I've missed you."

"You have?" Sadie asks, looking surprised.

"Of course. You're my bestie. Remember?"

I hear someone scoff on the other side of the room. I'm going to assume it's Victoria, because the rest of my family knows Laura. We've accepted that she's a free spirit and a people person. So, yes. It had to be Victoria.

Sadie giggles. "I remember."

"Good. Now, let's all sit down so Charles can tell us his big news."

Oh, great. This all would have been so much easier if Laura had already blabbed to the rest of the family.

"Come on, people." Laura swings her arms, motioning for all of us to move closer. "Let's gather in this large seating area."

I quickly pull Sadie down into a loveseat and watch as my family slowly moves into other chairs and sofas all surrounding a large stone coffee table. Once everyone is seated, they slowly start to turn their heads to face me. Fuck. Clearing my throat, I smile. "Good to see all of you."

There are mumbles but not enough to require me to stop.

"Well." I pat Sadie's hand. "I guess I'll just say it."

I pause. Because this is damn nerve-wracking.

"Spit it out, bro," says Cortland. Of course.

So I do. I spit it out. "We're pregnant."

I think Mother took a sip of her drink at the wrong moment, because it ended up all over the stone table and a little on Victoria's shoes.

"Pregnant?" she says, sitting stiffly on the wingback side chair.

"Right on," chuckles Cortland. "It'll be fun to have a little rug rat running around. Stir some shit up."

"Cortland," snaps my mother.

"What? I'm serious. You all are boring as hell." He looks at Laura. "Not you, Gran. You're the bomb." Then he looks at Sadie. "Sadie, you're not boring either. At. All."

Sadie blushes as Laura responds, "Thank you, Cortland,"

"Charles." My father clears his throat. "Let me ask the question we're all thinking."

Shit.

"Son? Was this..." He pauses. "Planned?"

Sadie is about to say something, but I speak first, "No. But we're very happy about it." I look at Sadie. "Aren't we, darling?"

Sadie nods. Still speechless.

"You just met," spits Victoria. "Are you sure it's yours, Charles?"

"Victoria." I look at my mother and then scowl at Victoria. "If you're asking if we've had a paternity test, we haven't."

"But you will?" asks my father tentatively.

"We don't need one," I say angrily. "Jesus." I run my hand through my hair. I'm nearly ready to pull it out. I look over at Sadie. I don't want to answer that without her on board. She takes this one.

"As soon as I'm far enough along and it's safe, we'll have a paternity test. But let me reassure—"

"Really?" snaps Victoria. "You're kidding right?" She looks at my mother. "You're just going to let her do this?" Victoria turns to me. "Charles. This is ridiculous. You can't be serious about this... this *baker*."

She says "baker" like it's a dirty word or the oldest profession in the world.

I shake my head adamantly.

"Ha!" scoffs Victoria. "Emily assured me you were ready to settle down and that I was perfect for you. Hell, your mother convinced me to come along on this trip—that you were finally going to do something about it." Sadie wiggles her hand free from mine. I sense her pulling away.

"Sadie. It's not—"

"I need some air. It'll give you all a chance to talk amongst yourselves."

"Good idea. I'll go with you, sis," Cortland says, jumping up from his spot on the sofa.

"Cort—" I attempt to stop him, but why bother? It's probably best she not witness this shitshow. As the two of them walk out the door, Cortland points her toward the back of the house.

"So." Victoria stands with her hands on her narrow hips. "You can't deny there's something between us, Charles."

Yes, I can. I stand as well. "Victoria, you and I have never dated—were never a couple. Why would you believe I'd suddenly want that with you?"

"Be-because. We're perfect for each other."

"Mother?" I arch my brow her way. "I'm a thirty-two-year-old man. A physician. Why on earth would you think you could choose my partner?"

"It wasn't like that, dear."

"Sure, it was." Victoria interrupts my mother. Something you definitely don't do.

"Victoria. Enough." See? Now my mother is angry. Angry Emily Ashbury is a force you don't want to reckon with.

"But, Mother," Victoria whines.

"Mother?" I stare at my mom. Her face says it all. She *did* fill Victoria's head with dreams of marriage. "She calls you mother?" I start to chuckle. "Why would you do this? Were you afraid I'd never figure this out for myself?"

"You're not getting any younger."

"I'm thirty-two."

"And you're not getting any younger. I want grandchildren."

I'm taken completely aback by that. "Since when?"

"Since her friend Clarice Boudon started having them," my dad answers for me.

"Well, you're in luck." I smirk. I'm feeling a little cocky right now. "Congratulations, Grandmother Ashbury."

Laura snorts.

Then, my mother does something I haven't seen in a long, long time. She smiles. "I know."

"So, you're happy about this news?"

"Thrilled." She's beaming. Hell, her teeth are showing. "But I believe I'd prefer to be called Nana Ashbury or better yet, Grand-mere."

Laura snorts again.

"Mo— Emily, you can't be serious," Victoria spews angrily.

"Vicky, you'll be fine." Laura smirks. "There's still Cortland."

That's it. I can't help it—I laugh. I let the laugh come from my chest. "Victoria and Cortland?" I bend, placing my hand over my stomach, it's so damn funny. Cortland would eat her alive.

"Go to hell," Victoria says angrily as she stomps toward the door. "I'm leaving." She waits for one of us to say something, maybe try to stop her, but when no one does, she stomps her heeled foot. "Fine. I'll call a cab."

"Oh, no, Vicky." What the hell? Is Laura trying to stop her?

"What?" Victoria looks back at our matriarch expectantly.

"Don't call a cab. I'll have Glo give you a ride to the airport."

Victoria makes a screeching sound as she approaches the steps leading to the upper level. Her stiletto-heeled shoes stomp so loudly on the stone steps, I swear I feel the house move.

As soon as Victoria leaves, Mother stands and approaches me. "So... Sadie?"

"Yes." I'm not sure what her question is.

"You're going to marry her?"

"That's my plan. I haven't mentioned it to her yet, but I'm going into this with that expectation." I watch her face. She appears to be pleased with my answer, because that smile has reemerged.

My dad stands. Approaching me, he raises his hand, "Congratulations, son. I'm proud of you. I'm looking forward to... what did Cortland say? Having a rug rat running about." Dad chuckles. "It's been a long time since we've had a baby around."

"We'll have a paternity test," Sadie says as she comes up behind me.

Cortland is nowhere to be found. Lucky bastard.

"No." My mother sighs as she walks to Sadie. "I trust Charles to know what he's doing, and while I don't know you, Sadie, I'd like to get to know you. I hope you'll give me a chance."

I tug on Sadie's hand, giving it a squeeze.

"Of course, Mrs. Ashbury."

"I think you'd better start calling me Mother."

I watch Sadie closely. My mother doesn't know the significance of that statement. Sadie's eyes glisten. "Thank you. My mom died when I was seven."

My mother's face falls. "Oh, dear. I'm so sorry." We all watch as my mother reaches out with both arms and hugs Sadie. The entire room goes silent. Mother's arms are stiff but pliable. It's a start.

Leaning away from my mom for a moment, Sadie says, "It would mean a lot to me to call you Mom, especially since you'll be Peanut's nana." It's then that Sadie takes the opportunity to show Emily Ashbury how it's done. Wrapping my mom up in a tight hug, I see Sadie whisper something in my mother's ear. Then she smiles. Not my girl. She's always smiling. No, what's shocking is the beaming smile on my mother's face. And it's a real one. Again. Three times in one night. It's got to be a record.

"Who the hell is Peanut?" asks my father.

I chuckle. "That's our current name for the baby."

"Sweet." Oh, great. Cortland is back. "Peanut is an awesome name."

"That won't be the baby's actual name." Mother looks at Sadie. "Right?"

"Right." Sadie giggles.

"I'm calling the baby Peanut," says a defiant Cortland. "Peanut Ashbury. I love it."

"Oh, dear." Apparently my mom isn't on board with Peanut.

She'll have to get used to it, because Cortland wasn't teasing; I'm sure of that.

CHAPTER TWENTY-SEVEN

Laura

THE MINUTE I met Sadie (the woman formerly known as Rachel) I knew two things. One, she was special. Special in a way that made me want to know her. I could see fire in her eyes, and not like the fire you see in elitist debutantes like Victoria. That kind of fire is greed. No, Sadie's fire was for life, for hard work, for family, and for love. I could also tell her heart was broken. But in her sadness was determination to move forward. Okay, you may think I'm full of shit. Go ahead. But when you get to be my age, you can tell things about people.

The second thing I knew? She'd be perfect for Charles. That boy—or man, I should say—has only done what is right and proper his entire life. I'm sure he's had lovers and flings, but he's never given himself permission to live. He's the family mediator, the calm voice of reason, and the one who swoops in to save the day. This man, our hero, is surrounded by crazy, free spirits like Cortland and me, as well as people like his mother, who's emotionless most of the time, and his father, my son, who is really only interested in golf and the stock exchange. B-o-r-i-n-g.

But Charles is different. He's interest*ing*, of course. But more importantly, he's interest*ed*—in many things outside of our foo-foo lifestyle. He's a world-renowned surgeon. I suspect Sadie knows nothing about his reputation and client list. He's no bragger. Charles takes joy in things like movies, traveling, and fitness. I also know he has wanted a family of his own for as long as I can remember. Hell, he was Cortland's number one fan growing up. Charles took him everywhere and Cortland adored him. The little rascal thought Charles hung the moon. He still does.

When I met my sad new friend Sadie, I knew that those two people needed each other. Sadie needed to see that there are other fish in the sea, and Charles needed to see someone who needed him. Like that night at the disco. I knew poor Rachel was drinking away sadness. No judgment. That's why I leaned over to Charles that night at our table and said, "The poor girl. I think she's heartbroken. She has no one to take care of her tonight. It's too bad chivalry is dead."

And that did it. I knew my gallant hero of a grandson wouldn't be able to sit by and let Sadie née Rachel out of his sight. Charles was out of his chair in seconds. It didn't hurt that he couldn't take his eyes off her the entire night. Literally. He barely spoke to her, but he listened. He listened to everything she said. He laughed in the right places and smiled at her frequently. He was engaged at a level I'd never seen before. Certainly not with Victoria.

Ugh. Good riddance. My entire life, I've been surrounded by women, and men too, like that. I'm sick of it. Give me a million Sadies any day.

That's why I drove down to Sedona today, leaving the rest

of the fam in Page. There's no need for them to get involved in this cluster-you-know-what. Oh, hell. Clusterfuck. It's a goddamn clusterfuck. So I'm here, in an elevator on my way up to Winchester Commercial Investments and Consulting, to have a little chat with my old pal Bernice.

"Ha! Consulting, my ass." The Winchester family is the most notoriously unscrupulous group of people I've ever met. My father hated Andrew Winchester and the way he did business with a vengeance, referring to him as Andrew the Aberrant. And from the sounds of it, Bernice, now Beryl, has learned to be just as rotten. That's why when Charles told me the story of the lease and the silent partnership, I wasn't surprised. Sure, I felt terrible for Sadie having been duped like that but it's exactly the kind of thing the Winchesters have been doing forever. Hell, calling them consultants is an insult to consultants. Grifter is a much better word to describe the whole lot of them.

"Fucking Beryl," I mutter. I sense movement behind me. I'd like to tell you I'm alone in this shiny box, but I'm not. Several people, including my right-hand woman, Gloria, are with me. But I couldn't give a rat's ass what any of them think of me. I'm here for my bestie and my grandson.

When the elevators open, I step out into the lobby of Winchester's. God, it's atrociously decorated in lots of gold and brown. Pillars that look like they're covered in crackled gold leaf line the entryway. Inside reception hangs a chandelier that looks like it belongs in a baroque castle. The furniture is all covered in brown velvets, some with gold and brown brocade fabrics. It's fucking hideous. "Shit, Glo. It looks like one of those little ponies threw up in here. Who designed this place? Trump?"

"Laura," Gloria hisses. "Don't."

I laugh, but it sounds more like a cackle. I can't help it.

I step up to the reception desk and stare down at a girl who can't be more than twenty-one. "Welcome to WCIC, how can I help you, ma'am?"

I hate being called ma'am. "I'm here to see Bernice."

The little doe-eyed girl stares at me. "Bernice? I don't—"

"Oh, shit. Sorry. Beryl. I'm here to see Beryl."

She blinks at me some more. I'm starting to get annoyed by that look of pure unadulterated blankness.

"Hello?"

"D-do you have an appointment?"

I turn my head and look at Glo, giving her my trademark eye roll.

Gloria steps forward to take over because she knows I've lost patience with this entire process. "Please tell Mrs. Winchester that Laura Storrance-Ashbury is here to see her."

"Storrance?" Blink. Blink. Blink.

Jesus.

"As in Veggie Beef and Noodle?"

"Among other things." Lots and lots of other things.

Glo and I watch as our little doe picks up her phone. Holding her hand over the receiver, she whispers, "Storrance." Pause. "Yes." Pause. "Right." Setting the phone down, she smiles.

"Mrs. Winchester's assistant will be here in a moment."

"Awesome," I mutter. Turning to Glo, I say, "Can you believe this shitshow?"

It makes Gloria laugh, which I like very much. Gloria can be such a curmudgeon.

I search the lobby for a chair that doesn't look like it'll harm me with all of the jagged gold points and shit when I hear my name. "Mrs. Storrance?"

That's not my name, but I'll go with it. Spinning on my heels, I'm shocked to see a man. He's youngish, blond, and quite attractive. Holding his hand out, he approaches me with a bright smile. "Good afternoon. I'm Thomas. Would you like to follow me?"

Not really. "Sure thing, toots."

He chuckles, and I rather like him already.

Glo and I follow him down a long corridor, taking one turn after another. "Going down the rabbit hole, Glo. Only there's no Mad Hatter there, only Satan's mistress."

Thomas chuckles again. "I suppose that makes me the White Rabbit."

"Oh, I hope not. If that's the case, come work for me."

Thomas stops walking and turns to face me. In a low voice, he says, "If you have a card, I'll call you tomorrow."

"Glo." That's all I have to say, and she's got my card out of her bag and into Thomas's hand.

"Thank you." Thomas slides the card into his pocket, then leads us to a huge set of double doors. Double golden doors. "Garish," I mumble.

"Mm-hmm," says Thomas, only loud enough for me to hear. He lifts a large knocker on the door and taps it twice.

"A knocker?"

"Mm-hmm."

"Enter."

Thomas pushes both doors open and steps aside.

"Laura," Bernice says as she steps away from her desk.

If I told you it wasn't gold, would you believe me? No? I didn't think so.

"Bernice."

"Oh, you silly. I'm Beryl, remember?"

"Right." I step up to the set of chairs in front of her desk. Plopping my ass down, I set my purse on her desk. "Let's cut the shit, Beryl. I need you to do me a favor."

"A favor? *You* need a favor?"

I chuckle. "Well, maybe I'm doing you the favor."

Beryl sits her bony ass down in her throne and leans back, her eyes never leaving mine. "Enlighten me."

So I do. I tell her what I know about her duping my future granddaughter with the contract scam, and how she and her son have gone out of their way to stalk and harass Sadie, and then I tell her that my attorneys are currently looking into suing one Candy P. Cane and Andrew Winchester for destruction of property, pain and suffering, and whatever else they can think of. They're clever. They'll think of a few more things.

"Don't be ridiculous, Laura. We did none of those things."

I arch my brow, lean forward, and remove the documents I have in my bag. "Sadie isn't the only one you've done this to, Bernice. According to court documents, you've been a busy little swindler for years. So many lawsuits related to your real estate enterprises have been registered against you in Arizona alone. Strange, they never seem to make it to court, though. Always settled before that happens." I make a tsking sound. "And the non-disclosure agreements." I tsk again. "I'd hate for the word to get out how unscrupulous you are. That 'excellent reputation' you love to tout would be worthless."

Bernice is scowling. She seems unhappy. But I suspect that's just how she looks. "What do you want?" she snarls.

Finally. We're getting somewhere.

This day has been quite productive. Not only is Bernice going to get her comeuppance, (just wait and see), but I've got a new assistant in Thomas. I believe he's just jaded enough to work out. He'll fit right in.

CHAPTER TWENTY-EIGHT

SADIE

HOLDING up my glass of ice water with a lemon wedge, I say, "Ladies, thanks for meeting me. I've missed you all like cray-cray."

"Here, here," they all say in unison.

I'm out at Murphy's with my sisters, and it feels like it's been months since the last time we were together. It hasn't been; it's only been a few weeks since we all met here, plus they came to visit me at the hotel the other day.

The thing is, while I miss my siblings, I know they're always with me. I also know I can call or text them any time, day or night. Take tonight, for example. Charlie left for Los Angeles this morning, and the minute he walked out with his suitcase in hand, I felt lonely. Alone. So, I sent out a Palmer Sister alert and asked them all to meet me here for a dinner of wings, potato skins, and mozzarella sticks. That's our usual order anyway. Ordinarily, I'm the first to dig into spicy chicken wings, but,

195

thanks to morning sickness, just the idea makes me feel queasy. So I opt for a simple order of sweet potato fries with no salt. I hope Charlie would be proud of me for choosing a healthier option.

"Charlie's gone?" Lainie asks, interrupting my thoughts.

"He is. He'll be back in a few days."

"Then what?" Keely mutters as she bites into a hot mozzarella stick.

"Then what? What do you mean?"

"Then what? Are you getting hitched?"

Hitched? Shit. The thought hasn't entered my mind. Not yet anyway. "Not yet, but I think we're buying a house?"

"Are you asking us or telling us?" says Aggie with a giggle.

"I don't know. He wants to buy a house. Here in Page. For us."

I must have said the wrong thing. Or maybe it was the right thing. Either way, none of my sisters are speaking. Neither are they drinking or eating. They're gaping.

"What?"

"Where do we start?" Violet says in a startled voice. "Did he propose?"

Leave it to Violet to ask the one question I can't answer. I guess I can. "No."

"Oooh, Sadie's going to live in sin," Keely says in an annoyingly snooty singsong voice.

"Look. This is all moving so damn fast. One minute I see my life just me and Peanut...," I say, touching my stomach.

"Keep going, Sadie." Violet says, leaning in.

So I keep going. I tell them how fast this thing is going with Charlie. That I had feelings for him on the ship, but I assumed those feelings were all related to my breakup with Andrew. Like I was grasping at the first chance for me to feel like I wasn't to blame. Or maybe I just didn't want to feel bad about it and let it ruin the vacation I'd scrimped and saved for. "Is it possible to make it work when you know so little about each other?"

I'm asking all of my sisters that question, even though two of them fell in love in record time, to men they're both currently engaged to.

Aggie goes first. "When you know, you know."

"I thought I knew with Andrew."

"You thought he was your person, but, deep down, you knew he wasn't."

"Aggie, I'm not sure that's true."

"I tend to agree." Violet has been quite talkative tonight. "You used to work extra hard to make excuses for him. He never wanted to hang out with all of us. That should have been sign one that he wasn't your person, because your person would want you to be happy, and you could never be happy if your partner or spouse stayed home instead of attending Palmer family functions. Right?"

"Wow, that was a soliloquy, sis. Why so chatty?" chuckles Keely.

Violet shrugs and sips her water. Water again. I guess I should be happy I've got a drinking buddy. Two, if you count Lainie.

"Look." Lainie scoots up to the table to engage us all. "I get why you're confused. You're not only dealing with a new relationship, you're pregnant to boot."

Keely laughs. "To boot. I'm using that."

Shaking her head, Lainie continues, "My advice?"

I nod.

"I watched him with you. I saw him care for you. It wasn't fake or for our benefit. The guy has feelings for you. I also saw you, my sweet little sister. You look at him like he's your person."

"Her person?" Keely expression turns serious.

Lainie doesn't let Keely stop her. "Andrew...." She pauses like she's trying to figure out the right way to say it.

"Spit it out, Lainie," Aggie urges.

"Andrew was a douche. You took care of him. He never did anything for you. When you were sick, he stayed down in Sedona because he was afraid to catch it. But when he was sick, you took time out of your busy life to stay with him."

"Oh, right." Keely nods.

"He didn't support your career goals, saying he wanted you to move to Sedona and be a stay-at-home mom when you had kids."

"I know."

"It was always about Andrew and what Andrew wanted. Hell, last Christmas, what'd he give you?"

Oh, yeah. I forgot about that. "A barbeque grill."

"A barbeque grill." Lainie nods. "Can you have a grill at your apartment?"

"No."

"So, where is your grill now? At his place in Sedona?"

I blush at the memory. It was state of the art. Stainless steel with blue backlit LED safety knobs and internal halogen lights for nighttime grilling. It was one of those that hooked up to the natural gas line of your house. It had infrared burners and a meat probe. It was Andrew's dream grill. He talked about it incessantly until I unwrapped it on Christmas morning.

"Actually, it's sitting out on the walkway outside of Candy P. Cane's apartment."

"What? Why? Did he bring it back to you?" asks Violet.

"No." I learned that Andrew moved into Candy's place the hard way. When I went home today right after Charlie left, there was a moving van parked in the lot. A sense of excitement ran through me, thinking it was Candy moving out. But when I saw them bringing furniture up the steps to the apartment next to mine rather than the other way around, I knew. Besides, I recognized the grill in question as they rolled it out of the truck.

Sighing, I say it. "He moved in with her."

Agatha nearly chokes on a chicken wing. "Andrew? Andrew Winchester moved in with the stripper?"

"Apparently. I hid in my apartment and watched it happen through my blinds." After sneaking up the back staircase and slithering into my apartment, that is.

Keely snickers. "Beryl has got to be shitting her pants."

I shrug, because it didn't seem to bother her one way or the other. "No idea."

"Can he use it? At Candy's?"

"No. The complex doesn't allow grilling."

"Shit!" Keely shouts. "We should go get that fucking grill. You could use it at your new place. With Charlie."

One by one, each of our frowns turn upside down. Smiles appear around the table, and it makes me feel abso-fucking-lutely giddy.

"It's not stealing. It *is* mine."

"Damn straight it's yours," Keely says, slapping the table.

"It's huge," I warn.

"That's what she said."

"Violet!" We all start to laugh, and it continues until we've all finished our drinks and eaten the last appetizer from the table.

"What's the plan?" I ask Lainie.

She's got a call into her fiancé, Keeton, to see about borrowing a vehicle. "Eric has a pickup."

"Eric? His brother?" asks Violet nervously.

"One and the same."

When her phone chimes, she reads Keeton's text aloud. "Babe, Eric will meet you at Sadie's with the pickup in 10. Call Ian and tell him I'm picking him up."

"I can't believe we're doing this." I feel a shiver of excitement run up my spine. It's a good feeling. "Where are we going to store it?"

"In our garage. There's space behind Keeton's bikes. You can get it when you move."

"Are you sure?"

Lainie looks at me like I'm crazy. "Keeton won't mind. He loves you."

"He does?" I squeak. Why did that statement make me emotional?

"Aw, honey," Lainie says as she approaches me, wrapping me up in her arms. "Of course he loves you. He's told me more than once just this week that he's happy you met a man like Charlie."

I sniffle. "He did?" I look at her face. She wouldn't lie to me. "He likes Charlie?"

"He does. He thought he was a 'stand-up guy.' His words."

"Ian likes him too," says Aggie, getting into the hug. "Plus, he checks out."

I stare at Aggie.

"What? Ian called in a favor." I'm still staring, and she looks rather baffled. "You expect me to sit back and...?" She looks around the table. "It's our job, girls. It's what we do. It's what I do now."

And that's all it takes for all of us to burst into laughter.

"Bitches," Aggie mutters.

Once the laughter subsides, Keely picks the thread back up. "Dad thought Charlie was the bomb, Sadie."

I'm so glad. It makes me feel emotional to hear all of these people giving me love and saying such nice things about Charlie. "W-what about you guys? Your opinion means the world to me."

"We know," they all say, pressed up against me.

"We all thought he was special, Sades."

"And fucking hot." Leave it to Keely to give us some comedic relief.

"Come on, girls. Let's go get us a grill."

"Hells, yeah!" Keely shouts, raising her fist in the air. "Girl Power!"

"*Palmer* Girl Power," corrects Violet.

Exactly.

~

"OKAY, bitches, it's time for Operation: Grill Heist."

"My God, Keely. You're such a dork." I snort with a laugh. We're all standing in the parking lot waiting for Eric to show up with the pickup truck. I think we need to hurry. Andrew's car isn't here, which is good, but he could pull up any moment.

"What is the plan?" whispers Violet. She seems visibly nervous.

Rubbing my hand up and down her arm, I reassure her, "This isn't stealing, hon. That's *my* grill up there."

"Oh, um, I know. It's just...." Violet stops talking the minute two vehicles pull into the lot.

"Keeton's here," chimes Lainie. "Yay!"

"And he brought reinforcements," Agatha says happily as she skips, yes, that's what I said, skips over to Eric's truck, pulling open the passenger door as Ian slides out in front of her. He kisses her sweetly, and I watch, a little envious, as they whisper things to each other.

My hand is still on Vi's arm, and I feel her stiffen up the minute Eric Gustafson slides out of the truck. Something tickles my hand. Goose bumps. Violet just got goose bumps. Interesting.

As all three men approach, I smile. We've got reinforcements, and this is turning into a rather fun operation, as Keely said. The only thing missing? Or, the only person missing? Is Charlie. He should be here too.

Clearing my throat, I decide to stop my sad thoughts and enjoy this moment with my family. "Okay. The grill is up there." I point up to the third floor of the apartment building. The walkway is open, so they can all see the grill pushed up against the metal railing.

"That's a big sum-bitch," says Eric with a chuckle.

"It is. We——" I point to my sisters. "—would never be able to move it, so thanks for helping."

"We wouldn't expect you to move it, darlin'," Keeton says, smiling. "Especially in your condition."

I roll my eyes. Men. "So what's the plan?"

"You ladies stay here. We'll go get it." Keeton again.

"Okay, honey." Lainie leans up and kisses Keeton on the cheek.

I'm rolling my eyes so much my sockets are starting to hurt.

We watch as the three men take the steps up to my floor two at a time. It's dark on my landing. I need to call Parker about it, but for now it's a good thing, since we can barely see the men.

They start to move the grill, but then I see it stop suddenly. The men huddle together. Eric splits from the group and jogs down the stairs toward his truck. As he passes Violet, I watch his hand reach out and touch her back lightly. Violet becomes stiff as a board suddenly, and then I see the tiniest smile appear on her face. Something is going on with my baby sister. And I think his name is Eric.

We watch Eric root around in the back of his truck until he pulls out some big tool. Looking at Vi, Eric says, "Bolt cutter."

Violet releases a gust of air and the world's quietest giggle.

I'll be damned.

In minutes, the guys have the grill freed from its chains and they're carrying the monstrosity down the steps. It's like they're special ops or something; they're barely making a sound.

Once on level ground, the guys roll the grill to the back of Eric's truck, hoist it up, and secure it in place. The entire "operation" from start to finish took less than fifteen minutes.

"We'll store it in our garage, Sadie," says Keeton as he secures the last tie in place.

"Great." I smile at my future brother-in-law, then at Ian and Eric. "Thanks, guys."

"You'd better hit the road before the asshole gets home," Keely says quickly. "Or before the cops come." Surprisingly, she says that last sentence with much less venom than usual.

Before Eric hops in his truck, he turns back. When his eyes meet Vi's, he lifts his hand, giving her a tiny wave and a soft but sweet smile. "See you, Violet."

Violet nods nervously, looking around to see if anyone noticed.

It doesn't appear anyone else is aware, but I am. *I* noticed.

CHAPTER TWENTY-NINE

SADIE

"HEY, how long has it been since Andrew and Bitchy Beryl stopped into the bakery? It seems like forever," Polly says out of nowhere.

"Almost two weeks. I think Andrew heeded Officer Martelli's advice. I hope he stays away."

"Meow," Polly says from out of nowhere. In addition to her feline interjection, she uses her hands to make the motion of a cat scratching.

"What the hell?" I laugh.

"Meow. Kitty likes Officer Martelli."

"Who the hell is Kitty?" I don't want to know. Swear to God.

"Me. *I'm* Kitty." Polly sighs. "I love me some Officer Nick Martelli."

"Yeah, well, don't let Keely hear you say that."

"I know. She's definitely got a hard-on for cops. Why is that?"

I shrug. "It's been that way for years. I don't know if she had something happen in college or what."

Polly laughs, "Knowing Keely, she probably had one brush too many—and with that mouth of hers."

I nod. "No doubt."

"Oh, well." Polly sighs, "Someday my prince will come and all that bullshit."

I laugh. I can't help it. My bestie is hilarious. "Well, you've certainly got a certain Bostonian smitten."

Polly rolls her eyes. "Cortland Ashbury is just bored. He's far away from home and he's bored."

"I don't know him well enough to tell you that you're right, but the way he's been salivating around you like a puppy this week, I'd say it's more than boredom that keeps him coming back every single day."

"I can't let myself get caught up in him. He'll be gone soon."

Interesting. "You like him, though?"

"What's not to like?" She pauses. "Okay. He definitely spends more time on his hair than I do. Other than that, he's gorgeous, charming, funny, and he's got great taste in women." I get a wink after that.

"You should go out with him. He's asked you twice now. He even wrote you a poem."

Polly giggles. "He did."

"It was sweet."

Polly stops weighing dough. "*Your voice is as sweet as the treats you dispense....*"

"You memorized it?" I giggle.

"*My heart beats like a drum and the feeling is intense....*"

I stop working the dough to hear the rest.

"When I think of beauty, I see your face..." She pauses. *"All things considered, you're worth the chase."*

"That *was* pretty awesome."

Polly nods, giving me a shy smile. "No one has ever written me a poem before."

"Now someone has."

"He's leaving soon. Heading back to Boston," Polly says, sounding a little sad.

"He'll be back. He likes it here."

Polly's face becomes hard, neutral. "It'd never work out, Sadie. Guys like him...."

I wait for the rest but she's taking too long. "What about guys like him?"

"They don't keep girls like me. That's why I can't do it. I can't fall for him." She looks up at me, and I can see real pain in her eyes. "I have a feeling that man could break me."

Wow. *Wow.* My best friend, the boy-crazy girl that I love dearly, has finally met her match. The one that scares her. The one that makes her see that she's going to need to take a risk or two. That's terrifying. I know about that firsthand. Honestly, I don't know what Cortland's true intentions are—I don't know him well enough. But the little I've seen so far tells me he's not about to give up. Not yet. There must be something in the Ashbury DNA that makes them especially tenacious when faced with a challenge. In this case, the challenge is a woman.

"So, Charlie's been gone a week?" Polly asks, knowing damn well how long he's been gone.

"Changing the subject, I see. Yes. Six days." Charlie's patient encountered some complications after surgery, so he's still in Los Angeles.

"He'll be back tomorrow?"

"That's what he said." But he's said that a couple of times now.

"Are you still staying at Keely's?"

"Yeah. I didn't feel comfortable staying at the hotel alone, and I definitely didn't want to go back home. Not with Andrew and Candy next door."

"Yeah, sorry about that. Parker told me he was moving in, but with everything that was happening with you and Charlie and my working extra at the bakery, I hadn't had time to tell you. I thought it'd sound better face-to-face."

"No. It's okay. And I'm sorry you've had to work so much."

"Stop right there," she says, slapping a hunk of dough onto the table. "It's what besties are for. If the situation were reversed, you'd have done the same times ten."

"You're more than my bestie, Polls."

She winks at me as she plops down more bread dough on the scale.

"I still can't believe he moved in with her."

"But did you hear *why* he moved in with her?"

"No. I just assumed he wanted to." Andrew never does anything he doesn't want to do.

"I don't think he wanted to." Polly mumbles something I can't quite make out.

"What? Why not?"

"Well, two reasons. One has a lot to do with the other."

"What are you trying to tell me?"

"The rumor is... well, not rumor. Candy blabbed to Parker and, of course, he told me. Apparently he was over at her place trying to fix the toilet, *again.* Those kids of hers keep shoving shit down the toilet and flushing. This time it was some kind of action hero."

"Spit it out!" I shout. I could care less about Candy's bathroom issues.

"His mom kicked him out."

"What?!" I screech. "No way. She'd never. Not Andrew."

She looks at me and then down at the dough. "And they're looking for a larger apartment in the complex."

"Why?" I blink.

"They need another bedroom."

I blink more. *No.* "She's not."

"She is."

She's pregnant. Candy P. Cane is pregnant. "Wow." That hurts. A lot.

"That's why Beryl the Bitch kicked him out. She gave him an ultimatum."

I can't believe this. Any of it. Beryl Winchester thinks Andrew can do no wrong. She'd never cut him out of her life. Not completely.

"Is he still working for her?" Like I care.

"As of now, yes. But Beryl hasn't been speaking to him since he chose Candy over her."

"I can see that." I look down at the table. This entire thing depresses the hell out of me. He would have never chosen me over his mom, even if I was pregnant.

Polly must sense my mood, because she quickly says, "But look where he is now. He's stuck with Candy Cane for life. And you? You're so much better off. You're happier than I've ever seen you. You haven't puked all day."

I have, but I did it when she happened to be out on a delivery. I also haven't eaten. I've tried, but I just haven't had an appetite. But when I hear Charlie's voice in my head about eating healthy, I pick up a few grapes or carrots and eat them.

Polly's just trying to be optimistic. My morning sickness started back up with a vengeance the day Charlie left for California. I'm sure it was just a coincidence. No worries; I've been drinking water like it's, well, water, taking my vitamins, and resting as much as possible. That's not easy with a bakery to run, but I'm doing what I can. I lie down between orders for a few minutes here and there. Every bit helps.

"No. Good for them." I shrug.

"Do you really mean that?"

"No." I cough, then laugh. "Hell, no. Screw them."

That starts a round of giggles. First Polly loses it, then me. We laugh so hard we have to get tissues to wipe our eyes and blow our noses.

"Yeah," Polly says toward the end of our fit of laughter. "Fuck 'em."

And it starts again. Laughter really is the best medicine. I haven't felt this good since... since the last time I slept next to Charlie.

I sigh, thinking about being cuddled up next to him. In six years, I never felt that way about sleeping with Andrew. On the contrary, the man was a blanket thief and a bed hog. Not to mention he sweated so much I never wanted him to touch me. As soon as the sex was done, he rolled over to his side and fell asleep. The fact that I worked at the ass-crack of dawn bothered Sleeping Beauty so much he rarely stayed at my place.

"You love him, don't you?"

"Andrew?" I screech.

"No, dummy. Charlie. You're in love with him."

I stop kneading the dough I'm working with and stare at my friend. "I've given that question some thought, especially after the night at Murphy's with my sisters. I needed advice and since Lainie and Agatha have both fallen in insta-love recently, I thought it'd be wise to talk it out with them."

"What'd they say?"

"Well, let me think." I walk around the table to sit on a stool for a bit. Rest. I'm getting rest. "Lainie said that she fell in love with Keeton the day she met him."

"Jesus, who wouldn't? Have you seen him?" Polly says,

fanning herself.

I arch my brow at her. I'm not sure I like that she's pining for my sister's fiancé. "He's taken."

"No shit. He's like a caveman when it comes to your sister." In a faux manly voice, Polly says, "Mine. Lainie is mine."

I shrug. "Nothing wrong with him telling everyone. Besides, after all the crap that went down with Lainie's ex, I'm glad she's met someone who thinks she's the best thing since..." I pause, looking at our dough. "Since sliced bread."

"Har dee har har."

"Agatha's was more of a slow burn. I think it took her and Ian a month."

Polly chuckles. "Wow, they took forever."

"In comparison, yes. But I asked them how they knew."

"And?" This has piqued Polly's interest.

I shrugged. "They just said that they got chills when they were around each other. They couldn't stop thinking about each other when they were apart. You know, the usual."

"Did you ever have that feeling with Andrew?"

"Maybe at first. That's what scares me."

"You're not nineteen anymore, babe. You've lived. You can tell the difference between infatuation and love. I know you can."

"I know."

"So, are you? In love with Charlie?"

I look over at my friend. "I am. I think I fell for him on the ship right after I saw the video of him helping me on the dance floor. And I've missed him so much this week, it makes me feel sick. But, damn, Polly. It scares the bejesus out of me. What if I'm wrong again?"

"Don't be scared, beautiful. I've got you," says a deep voice somewhere behind me.

Turning quickly, I drop the dough onto the stainless steel

table and race to him, jumping into his arms. "Charlie! You're finally home."

"I am. I'm finally home, honey."

I kiss his face. All of it. Every inch. "I've missed you so much." I'm hugging him so damn tight he probably can't breathe.

"I missed you too. More than you'll ever know." He's whispering in my ear. "I love you, Sadie. So fucking much. I can't stand the thought of my life without you. Knowing I got to come home to you... Jesus. It was everything."

"Charlie." I sniffle. I'm crying. Who wouldn't after hearing those words from the man you love? "I love you too. I think I got sick the second you walked out the door. I've been a wreck."

Setting me down on the floor, he looks at me, concern written all over his face. He quickly checks me for dehydration, but I've been diligent about my water intake. "I'm okay. I've been drinking plenty of water, resting whenever I can, eating healthy." Whispering, I add, "I promise, baby."

His deep rumble starts in his chest. I feel it because I'm still pressed up against him. "Are you about done here?"

"She's done," yells Polly from the front of the shop. "I've got this. Go home."

I didn't even see her leave the room. Sneaky devil. "I'm done." I smile brightly. "You hungry?" Because suddenly, I'm starving.

"SO, ABOUT EARLIER," I say, right before I bite into some of Charlie's chicken piccata. We're finally having our dinner at Giovanni's. I'd almost rather be at his hotel, but hunger won out over that. No worries, we can go home right afterwards. Both of our plates are in the center of the table so we can share. In less than a week, I've shown him the uncouth way to share a meal at a restaurant. He's very malleable when it comes to new ideas. At least he is here in Page. I suspect if we're ever in Boston at some fancy-ass restaurant, he'd be resistant to sharing plates. It's okay. I'll take this.

"What about earlier?"

I know he knows what I'm referring to. It's sort of an elephant in the room kind of thing. "At the bakery."

"At the bakery?" He reaches out with his fork to cut off a slice of my lasagna. Leaning over the table, he slides the cheesy morsel in his mouth.

"Charlie. You know what I mean. Did you mean all of that back there?"

Placing his fork on the table, Charlie reaches his hand out until he's got one of mine in his. "Sweetheart. I did. But I'm not going to lie; I'm scared too. I'm about to be a father. But I've had over two months to prepare myself to the idea of you and me. It was all I thought about."

"It was?"

"It was. You were. It's why I had to find you. To see."

"To see if you liked me?" I hope he corrects me.

"I knew I liked you. What's not to like? You dance like nobody's watching."

I release a nervous laugh and slap at his hand. "Shush. That was embarrassing."

"Hey, I'll dance with you anywhere, anytime." I roll my eyes just as he says, "Maybe at our wedding."

"Charlie."

"I know. Too fast."

"A little. I'm not opposed to the idea, but I need more time."

"I understand. But I'm hoping you like the idea of moving forward. I'd like us to house hunt this week. Are you available at all during the day?"

He just said so much right then. "House hunt?" I knew it was coming.

"House hunt."

I nod slowly. "I can pop out of the bakery throughout the day. Just let me know when you've got appointments."

"The first one is at ten in the morning. She wants to show us three places."

"Charlie, we haven't even talked budget yet. Besides, I'm not sure what's happening with the bakery and the Winchesters. What if I'm out of a job?"

"Then we'll figure it out. It's what couples do. We'll work together. We'll figure it out."

"Okay. That's fair, but we haven't talked price range. I don't want to walk into a place and fall in love with it only to find out it's a gazillion dollars."

"Fair enough. If we find a place, my mom and Laura want to check it out."

"Your mom and Laura? I thought they left today." They've been regular fixtures at the bakery this week. The entire family has sampled just about everything I make. Last I heard, they were flying out together.

"The others left. Mom and Laura wanted to take you shopping for baby gear."

"Baby gear," I say sort of breathlessly. "I hadn't given that any thought yet." I'll need to start a list. Maybe get with Lainie to see what she's going to get.

Reaching across the table, Charlie takes my hand in his. "You just found out, and we've got plenty of time."

"Did you know Cortland likes it here? Well, I think he likes Polly." I smile.

Charlie nods. "He told me he never wanted to leave." Realizing my last statement, Charlie asks, "Polly?"

"It appears so."

"I can see that. She's spunky and *very* attractive."

I give him my arched brow.

"Not as attractive as you. You know how I feel about you."

"Yeah, yeah. It was sort of cute. Cortland walked into the bakery and stopped in his tracks when he caught a glimpse of the blonde bombshell. He smiled like he'd just won the lottery. As he approached, he looked at her name badge and sang, 'Well, hello, Polly.'"

"Like the movie?"

"Yep. He even sang it."

"Idiot."

"Polly nearly expired when he asked her out. She said no of course. She always says no. She wants them to work for it. But Cortland came back every day, bringing her flowers, knick-knacks, and one day he brought her a handwritten poem."

Charlie's turn to choke. "A poem?"

"Yep. And it wasn't bad."

"There must be something there. I think he's flying back in a day or two. He wanted to bring back a few more of his things."

"Serious? Do you think he'll stay? What will he do? Does he have a job?"

Charlie chuckles, then rolls his eyes. "He works with Laura."

"Doing?"

"Her bidding. Whatever she wants him to do. He travels a lot."

"Has he always done that?"

"Since he graduated from Harvard Law, yes."

"Law school!?" I nearly choke. Why does that shock me? The Ashbury gene pool must have extra brain-DNA. Is that a thing? I should ask Violet. She's *our* resident smarty-pants.

"You wouldn't know it by talking to him, but the kid is very bright."

"Apparently." Hmm, interesting.

The news that the three of them are going to be here for a while gives me an idea. "Do you think your father and Catherine will come back? I'd like to have a get-together with my family. They should all meet."

Charlie gives me a beaming smile. "They'd love that. *I'd* love that, Sadie. Our families are going to spend lots of time together; we might as well introduce them sooner rather than later."

Well, I'll be... I'm surprised he's so amenable to the idea. I hate to compare him to Andrew again, but Beryl and Andrew never wanted to spend time with my family. I guess it could still happen with Charlie's crew. Once they meet my clan, they may recoil.

After taking my last bite of lasagna, I wipe my mouth. "Your family—they've been to the bakery every day."

"I know." He chuckles. "Mom said she's gained five pounds."

She could stand to gain five pounds. Or ten.

"My entire family is in love with your treats. Dad thinks you could go national."

"No way. I'm busy enough as it is. It's sweet of him to say, though."

"Sweet? He's serious. He sees dollar signs, thanks to your chocolate-covered cherry cupcakes."

I smile proudly. "Those are new."

Looking at me across the table, he winks, "I can't wait to bite into your goodies."

My eyes are hooded just thinking about him with my goodies. "What are we waiting for?"

"Check!" Charlie says a tad too loudly, which gives me the giggles.

God, I'm happy.

CHAPTER THIRTY

SADIE

"SO, kiddos, tell me about the houses you looked at today," Laura says, sitting across from Charlie and me at the kitchen table in her huge eat-in kitchen. "Did you find one you both liked?"

I'm enjoying a nice cup of green tea while Charlie sips on an amber cocktail of some sort. Laura didn't want to drink alone. "Well. The first house was filled with dead animals."

"Dead animals? What the hell?" cackles Laura.

Charlie describes the scene. "Taxidermic animals. Birds, antelope, and there was even a bobcat on the fireplace mantel."

"Ooh, there was a fireplace?" asks Emily, entering the kitchen from the living room. "I love fireplaces."

"Is that one out?" Laura asks.

"It is. Besides the entire place being covered in deceased animals, it was way over budget."

"Budget?" Laura asks, looking over at her daughter-in-law, then back at us.

What? She doesn't know what that is? I explain, "A budget is something you use when you're shopping. It's a limit to the amount of money you can spend."

"Smart ass," Laura says with a chuckle. "All I meant was, why do you have a budget?"

I think she's seriously asking. "Because."

"Because why, my dear?" Emily's turn to confuse me. "Charles?"

I don't want to put him on the spot. "I'm paying half, so we can't go crazy. I have a business to run." For now.

"What the hell are you talking about?" Laura actually sounds upset.

"What do you mean, what am I talking about?" I set my teacup down onto the pretty saucer. I need to start serving tea in pretty cups at the bakery.

Emily reaches over and pats Laura's hand. "She means, my dear, that you don't have to worry about money anymore. Tell her, Charles."

"I've mentioned it. But I respect Sadie's desire to keep costs down. We have a baby to think about."

Laura starts to laugh. Emily joins in, then says, "She doesn't know your net worth, does she, Charles?"

I don't need to know. "I know you're all wealthy, but I'm not, and I will not go into a relationship with Charlie feeling like I'm not an equal partner in this thing. I want our first home together can be something we do together. I don't need a man to buy a house *for* me. I just want Charlie to buy a home *with* me. And to accomplish that, it will need to be fairly modest."

"Oh, sweetie." Emily turns to pat my hand. I think the ladies are getting tipsy. Emily's starting to slur a little. "He's head over heels for you. He'll do whatever you want, but don't let that stubborn pride keep you from getting a home you can live in long-term. Something with extra rooms for your in-laws," she winks.

"Mother." Charlie decides to enter the fray.

Okay. I know they mean well, but this is making me uncomfortable. "I appreciate what you're saying, and I'm honest to goodness not trying to make it sound like I don't like money, I just don't want more house than we need. There's no need to go overboard on a house. It's a home I want; it doesn't matter how big it is for it to work."

"Oh, my sweet girl." Emily actually sounds sincere. She even reaches out and touches my cheek. "Now I get it."

What does she get? "What?"

"I get what Charles sees in you."

She didn't before? Awesome.

"You're the real thing."

Of course I'm real. What does she think I am? A robot? Ooh, or a nymph. I'd love to be a nymph.

"What Emily is trying to say, Sadie, is that you're authentic."

"What else would I be?" I mean, seriously.

"You'd be surprised," quips Laura.

I turn to Emily, who looks like she may cry. "Are you okay?"

"Yes, my dear. I couldn't be happier. Charles is a special man. I should never have tried to push Victoria and Charles together."

"No shit," mutters Laura.

I can sense Charlie fidgeting next to me. Tipsy Emily is letting it all hang out. "Why did you?" I have to know the answer.

"Of all my children, Charlie needed his own family. He's always wanted children." She looks at her son, then touches his cheek. "Isn't that right, Charlie?"

Stiffly, Charlie says, "I want a family, yes."

Emily's not done. "He needs someone to care for, but I want someone who'll care for *him* too."

Laura scoffs. "And you thought that was Victoria?"

"I suppose I did." Turning to me, she smiles. "But you're perfect for him, Sadie."

I look over at my man. "*He's* perfect."

Laura mumbles, "No man is perfect, sweetie. Trust me."

"Laura's right about that." Charlie smirks.

"Alright, enough of that. Tell us about houses two and three."

So, I do. I tell them that the second house was a Tudor style that I didn't like but that I thought Aggie and Ian would like. With the realtor's okay, I called Agatha and invited her to see it. "They loved it. They're putting in an offer this afternoon."

"Wonderful. Good news for the Palmer girls."

I nod. "So, house three?"

"Spill the beans." Laura is such a dork.

"When we pulled up to the house, I knew it was over budget."

"How did you know?"

I point toward the front door. "Because it's across the street."

"Oh." Laura chuckles. "Most likely over budget then."

"I told her it was a foreclosure and in need of repairs, so the price was within the budget."

I roll my eyes. "I told him if that was the case, renovations would blow the budget out of the park."

"What did you say, Charles?" Emily asks.

"I said, 'Don't worry. I have money.'"

Laura interjects, "He does, Sadie. Lots of it."

"I know!" I shout, then laugh.

Both women chuckle as they sip their cocktails, no doubt

waiting for the rest of the story.

"Then what happened?"

"We had a fight. We said stuff."

"Like?" Emily is rather nosey.

Charlie answers that one, "I told her she needed to try to get past it because I'm probably going to get richer."

That gets the ladies laughing again.

He continues, "I also explained how important it was for me to find a home we can grow into. Oh," he holds up one finger, "And how much I love D.I.Y. projects."

That gets the ladies laughing again. "Since when?" asks Laura.

That comment seems to hurt Charlies because I can see his face flush pink. "Always. I've always wanted to fix up a place."

Emily looks at me with a very serious expression. "Sadie, marriage isn't easy. It's going to take compromise, love, and caring." She smirks, "And a whole lot of patience if you let Charles remodel your home."

That one makes me smile. Looking over at Charlie, I wink at him. "I've got faith that he can do anything he sets his mind too. Besides," I reach out and run my hand over his, "I'm handy and so is my dad. Doing home projects together sounds fun."

"We'll be together. We'll figure it out," Charlie says softly. "I love you. You love me. We're going to love Peanut with all our hearts. We don't need anything else. Not a fancy house or cars. Just us."

"And our families."

Charlie smiles. "And our families."

"I've got it!" shouts Laura.

Charlie and I turn to look at her. What has she got?

"Live here."

"No," Charlie and I say simultaneously.

"Why the hell not?"

I let Charlie take the lead.

"Because—" We look at each other. "We put an offer on the place across the street."

"Serious?" Laura jumps out of her seat and races around the table. Well, "races" is probably not accurate. The woman *is* seventy-seven. She *scurries* around the table and grabs both of us for a "group hug." Her words.

I look up at Charlie and smile. "Serious. It was perfect. The kitchen was as big as this one. It needs work but nothing that we can't do ourselves in time."

The thing is, I love the house. It isn't as big as I thought it would be from the street but still huge in comparison to my apartment. It's a sprawling ranch-style house of just over two thousand square feet. Charlie is right—it's not in great shape, and the decor is from 1970, but the layout is good. There is a great room but no living room to speak of, which is fine with me. Those formal rooms are a waste of space, in my book. It has four bedrooms and four and a half baths and a large dining room just off the kitchen I've ever seen. It's not up-to-date by any means, but it was designed for a real cook. The sink, stove (plus a set of double ovens on the wall), and refrigerator are close together, which makes cooking more efficient. The countertops span the entire circumference of the room, and there's a huge island in the middle of the room that's almost as big as my work surface at the shop. There is enough storage for all of my home baking equipment. And the best thing? The view. The kitchen windows overlook Lake Powell. Which means my mom will be with me, in spirit, whenever I'm in that room.

Laura smiles slyly. "Why did you give in, Sadie?"

"The kitchen." I smirk. "And I just couldn't picture Charlie in a two-bedroom ranch with one bath. Plus, we'll be right across the street from Ashbury central."

"So true, my dear. So true."

CHAPTER THIRTY-ONE

Charlie

GOD, I'm terrified. I knew Laura was up to something the minute I told her about Beryl Winchester. Now she's tasked me with telling Sadie the story. Correction—Laura handed me a large manila envelope before she and Emily left for home. They're coming back next week to shop for the nursery. While I know what Laura did, I've no idea how Sadie will react. She's weird about money. Once she finds out what Laura did, will she take off, leave me? I guess I'll find out in a few minutes.

Sitting at a table near the front window of Sadie Cakes Bakery, I wait for Sadie to return from a delivery. The bell above the door jingles, and I quickly turn to see Sadie enter. She's all smiles. Maybe she's thinking about last night. I know my mind has gone back to that several times this morning. My God, did I ever hit the jackpot. No, I'm not talking about how amazing she is in bed. I'm referring to the fact that she's the entire package. She's gorgeous, but that has nothing to do with it either. It's her heart. It's warm and loving, and I get to have a piece of that. Hopefully forever. But when she hears this from Laura, she may just end things.

God, I'm nervous.

I watch her approach and smile. She's beautiful today in her tight legging things and a Sadie Cakes T-shirt. Her hair is pulled back into a high ponytail, and her face is completely free of any makeup. She doesn't need it. Her loveliness is natural.

"Hey, Charlie." Sadie leans down and kisses my lips. "Can I get you anything from the case?"

"I should say no, but I can't. I'll have a cupcake. Surprise me."

"Anything to drink?"

"Coffee, please."

"I got you, babe."

Damn. I love her.

Once we're settled with our drinks and sweets, I hold my breath as I hand Sadie the envelope.

"What's this?"

"I'm not exactly sure of the contents. Laura wanted me to give it to you."

"Ooh, ominous."

Turning the envelope in her hand, she slowly lifts the flap. I lean in. God, I'm terrified.

Sadie slowly opens the envelope and pulls out a stack of papers. She reads the front page. At least I think she's reading it. She's just staring actually. When she flips that page over and places it on her lap, I watch her read the second page. This goes on for an interminable amount of time. Until I see it. A tear. One lonely tear slides down my beautiful girl's face. Shit. Shit. Shit.

"Sadie?" I say leaning forward.

She placed the papers gently on the table. I look first at

them, then back at Sadie. Holding my breath, I watch Sadie's mouth open.

"Laura bought Sadie Cakes." She's not asking a question.

I start to speak, but she interrupts. "For me."

I nod. I want to tell her I had nothing to do with it, but that's not true.

Sadie smiles, holding up page one of the documents for me to see. It's not a legal form; it's a letter. I take it in hand and read:

My dearest Sadie,

My grandson is worried sick you're going to be angry with him over all of this, but rest assured, he didn't put me up to any of this. Although I'm sure he won't mind my devious behavior. It was necessary and I'll tell you why. There are several reasons, actually. So, here goes…

One. I love you, dear girl. You're part of my family. You were even before Charles knocked you up. Two. You're one of the sweetest people I've ever met, and you didn't deserve that bullshit from Bernice and her asshole son. Three. I fucking hate Beryl Winchester. Period. My father hated Andrew Winchester. They've been cheating people forever, and I couldn't let her do it to you.

So I did something that may anger you. I purchased the building from Beryl. It now belongs to you and to one "Peanut" Palmer-Ashbury. I know you had a dream of opening this bakery with your mother and, sadly, that wish couldn't be fulfilled. So, I propose a new wish. That you and your daughter or son carry on that tradition together. You now own everything associated with your business. I've also started a small fund for Peanut to use later on in his or her life to invest in the business, or for anything else his or her heart desires.

Please don't be angry. It makes me happy to make you happy. So don't deprive an old woman of her joy.

Love,
Lauralai Marybeth Storrance-Ashbury

"WOW."

"You didn't know?"

"I knew she handled Beryl. I knew she bought the building."

"For me."

"For you." *God, please don't be angry.*

"Okay."

"Okay? You're not angry?"

Sadie places her palm over her belly. "She said it's for Peanut and me. How can I say no to that?"

She can't. I stand up, walk around the table, and kneel in front of my girl, placing my hands on her knees. "If it's any consolation, Laura makes that amount of money about every fifteen minutes thanks to all of her other ventures."

I get a big smile. "Yeah, that does help." Blinking, she adds, "How much damn money does she have?"

"You don't want to know."

"I do."

"Let's put this this way." I look into her eyes. "She could probably buy a mid-sized country."

Sadie's head flops forward. Her shoulders begin to shake. She's laughing? "Jesus. I can't believe I'm marrying into that."

"Marrying?"

She leans in and kisses my lips. "Eventually. When we're both ready."

Soon, then. "I'm ready whenever you are. Just say the word."

"Good to know." Sadie kisses me quickly as she stands up. "I've got work to do. Wanna help?"

"Sure. For a little while. I've got some errands to run in about an hour."

"Errands?"

"It's a surprise."

"Oh?"

"I'll tell you about it tonight. Shall we get takeout?"

"I guess." She shrugs. "I can't wait to move into our house. I'll be able to cook."

"We could go to your apart—"

"No. Andrew and Candy are next door. It's weird."

"You're letting them keep you from your own home? You're giving them an awful lot of power."

She's quiet. Just staring at me. "That's true." Sliding her hands into her apron pocket, she leans back on her heels. "Okay. Let's check out of the hotel and stay at my place."

"Good."

Turning away, she mumbles, "If Andrew asks about a grill, play dumb."

Huh? "Do I want to know why that is?"

"Probably not, but I'll tell you back here." She motions toward the back of the bakery."

"Great. I can't wait to hear this story." I follow her back into her work room. "Show me the cake, darling."

Sadie laughs, and it sounds beautiful. "Let me give Laura a call. I need to thank her."

"Sounds good."

CHAPTER THIRTY-TWO

SADIE

"I'VE GOT good news and bad news. Which do you want first?"

Charlie and I are sitting on my sofa eating the dinner I prepared in my own kitchen. Something we've done for the last five days, ever since we checked out of the hotel into Chez Sadie. Dinner is nothing fancy, just some stir-fry chicken and veggies. But at least it's not room service.

"Bad news." I like the idea of the good news blocking out the bad.

"I've got to leave again the day after tomorrow."

"The NBA player?"

"No. NFL player this time. In Denver."

I do my best to keep my face from showing how I really feel. Sad. I feel sad. And already lonely. "Okay." *Perk up, remember there's good news.* "And? The good news?"

He motions for me to sit on my sofa. "I've got two pieces of good news, actually." I wiggle in my seat. The anticipation is killing me. "The bank agreed to a fast closing."

"So you greased some wheels?" Money talks, after all.

"No grease required. They were anxious to get it off their books."

"What's the other good news?"

"I talked to the contractor your dad recommended. He said he can start work as soon as we get the keys."

"Really?" I squeak. "So, we could maybe, possibly move in at the end of the month-ish?"

"Ish. I gave them our punch list."

I just learned what a punch list is. If you don't know, it's a list of work a general contractor must complete prior to final payment. But in our case, it needs to be done before we can step foot into the place. "So, the roof repair, new air conditioner..."

"The water heater, the heat pump, and electric heater."

"That list keeps growing."

Ignoring me, he adds, "They're going to tear out the shag carpet for us and get the wallpaper off the walls in the kitchen, bathrooms, living room, dining room, and the master bedroom."

The wallpaper in the place was pretty groovy. Some of it I liked, but it's peeling badly in all the rooms, so it has to go.

"Don't forget about the wall of mirrors in the dining room."

"How could I forget?"

"Hey, how do they do that? It's seven years bad luck to break a mirror."

Charlie chuckles. "I think there's an exception to the rule when you're renovating."

I know he's making that up. "You're making that up."

Charlie sets his plate on my coffee table and scoots closer to me. Taking my plate, he sets it next to his. He runs his finger along my cheek, pushing back a lock of my hair. I love it when he does that. "I have one more bit of news."

"Good news?" Please be good news.

"I think so."

I wait as he slides his hand down my arm until he's holding mine. "I spoke to Sam McCormick."

"Dr. McCormick?"

"One and the same."

"And? Is this about me? Peanut?"

"Not directly."

I pull away from him. He's making me nervous and a little irritated. "Spit it out."

"I'm nearly positive I'm going to set up a practice here in Page."

"An orthopedic practice?"

"Yes. Or sorts."

"Of sorts? What does that mean? Would you still need to travel?"

"Some. For emergency surgery, I'd fly to the patient, but the idea here would be to create a private surgery and rehab center."

"So, your patients would stay here? In Page?"

Charlie nods. "They would. That's another area we'll need to address. My patients, mostly athletes, would expect five-star accommodations. We'll work that out later. The most interesting part of this will be that it'll be physically attached to Dr. McCormick's clinic, since there's a surgery center nearby."

"You'd need to build, right?"

"Not right away. There are empty offices in the same building. I'll need to renovate."

"That sounds expensive."

"Laura is going to invest a small portion."

I push away from him. I'm sort of getting sick of all the money. "Laura?"

"She wants to name the clinic after my grandfather."

"Uh-huh." I pick up the plate and march them into the

kitchen. I guess that's nice.

"Sadie?" he asks, following me into the kitchen. "If I do this, if *we* do this." He points to me and then back to himself. "I'll be here more than I'll be away."

Oh. "Really?"

"Really. There will be times I'll need to fly out for athletes who shouldn't travel, but the rest will be done here. I'd have more flexibility with my schedule, so I could take care of Peanut more often."

I place my palm on my stomach. "Why haven't you done this before? In Boston?"

"It'd always been something I considered. I guess it took meeting my person for me to pull the trigger."

"Y-your person?" He said it. "Do you mean that?"

"With all my heart."

I take the two steps needed to reach him and wrap my arms around his neck. He does the rest. With his hands on my bottom, he lifts me off the ground and onto my counter. "Ask me."

"Ask you what?" He blinks at me. "Oh, Right. Hang on. Don't move." He zips out of my kitchen and into my bedroom. *Our* bedroom. I hear rustling around, then footsteps. By the time he's back, standing in front of me, he's panting.

I remain silent. I know, hard to believe. He lifts me off the counter, back onto my feet. Then, the next thing I know, he's on his knee in front of me. "Sadie." He clears his throat. I can tell he's getting emotional. "I should wait and do something big—a grand gesture—but I won't pass up this opportunity."

I watch as a small black box is raised in front of me. With both of his hands, he pops the lid open, revealing the most beautiful little ring I've ever seen. It's a band. I don't know why I expected him to get me some huge rock but....

"I chose this sapphire ring because it reminded me of the

ocean. The place we met. Also, there's a chain in the bottom of the box so you can hang it around your neck while you're at work.

Okay, that did it. "So thoughtful. I love you so much, baby."

"Wait." He smiles. "I'm not done." Scooting a little closer, he continues, "You're my soul mate. I knew the second I laid eyes on you on the ship that you were the one. I thought I was having a heart attack." He laughs. "But it was just my heart telling me not to miss my chance."

I nod. I know what he means. I was just all confused with Andrew and everything.

"Sadie Palmer, will you do me the honor of marrying me?"

"I will. Of course I will." He's my person. No doubt in my mind.

Charlie stands, wrapping me in his arms as he gives me a deep, sweet kiss. Pulling away, he whispers, "I also bought you a three-carat rock, but I figured I'd ease you into that one."

"Charlie. Serious?"

"As a heart attack."

I reach for him so I can kiss him. "Thank you. You're the kindest, most thoughtful, caring, and sexy as fuck man I've ever met."

"Sexy, huh?"

"Definitely."

"Perhaps I should show you some new moves."

"New moves?"

Before I can say another word, I'm lifted off the ground and carried into our bedroom. Setting me on the floor, he says in a husky voice. "Clothes off. The only thing I want to see you wearing is my ring."

Oh, hell yes. A shiver runs up my back and all over my body. Goose bumps everywhere. I do as I'm told. Charlie's right. He has new moves, and they're awesome.

CHAPTER THIRTY-THREE

Charlie
Two months later...

"DEARLY BELOVED, we are assembled here in the presence of family and friends to celebrate the joining of this man and this woman in the unity of marriage."

How did this happen? One minute I find out he's smitten with Polly, and the next, this? This is so unlike my baby brother. In two short months, Cortland has moved everything he owns to Page, Arizona, all in the pursuit of Polly. I'd never seen the kid so determined. Well, kid is probably the wrong word. He's nearly thirty. It's just that he acts like a kid most of the time.

Okay, correction, he used to.

Ever since he met Polly, he's done all the grown-up things a guy should do. He bought a house down the street from our place. He hung his shingle, opening up his own law firm after getting approved to practice in Arizona. He's still working for Laura, but now he wants to help people—to take on clients who can't necessarily afford a lawyer. I don't think it'll be strictly pro-bono work but close. I'm impressed and humbled. I should consider doing more to help others—not just wealthy athletes. Polly has been a good influence on my brother.

Watching the ceremony, I can't help noticing how Polly's smile lights up the entire place. I peek over at my fiancée, Polly's maid of honor, and see her eyes wet with tears. Happy tears.

They promise to love, honor, and obey one another, only Polly changes hers up saying she'll love, honor, and talk things over with him before she makes up her own damn mind. That had the small crowd gathered in the outdoor wedding chuckling. I joined right in. Handing my brother her ring, he places it on her finger. I look at my Sadie again, winking from my spot beside my brother. What? Who else would be best man?

When it's time to kiss his bride, my brother goes all in. It's disgusting, really. I know my face is pinched with disgust, because when I look over at Sadie, she's bent over in laughter. At me. Her hand is resting on her slightly rounded belly, and I catch my breath. She's the most beautiful woman I've ever seen.

At almost five months along now, Sadie is over the morning sickness, thankfully. She's felt pretty good the last month or two. It's a good thing too. Getting the house ready for baby has been work. A labor of love but work. We moved in two weeks ago even though we only have one working bathroom. Don't ask. All I'll tell you is if you ever plan to renovate, expect the unexpected. My brick and mortar office will be fully up and running by the end of the year. That will mean much less travel for me and more for my clients. That's okay, most of them fly private, and the small Page airport will serve my business well.

I've been lucky. Sadie hasn't blown a gasket much at all. She's been busy with her bakery, shopping with Laura, Emily, and her sisters. The seven of them, eight with Polly, nine with

Catherine, when she can make it back, are all thick as thieves. They've all become incredibly close.

I watch as my brother walks hand-in-hand with his bride down the aisle. I reach for Sadie's hand and walk behind them out into the Page sunset. Our wedding is just around the corner. God, I can't wait to marry her. Leaning down, I kiss her cheek. "Our turn soon, my love."

"I know," she whispers. "I can't wait to marry you, baby."

Ah, hell. I'm the luckiest man on the planet. I kiss her hand as we follow the bride and groom into Laura's home for the reception. Time to celebrate.

Not just the wedding.

But, life.

A very good life.

The Palmer Sisters

Lainie

Agatha

Sadie

Cortland

Keely

Violet

Molly

Standalones

The Art of the Game

The Virginia Chronicles

One of a Kind

The Portrait Painter

Game Changer

Bedhead

Coming Soon: FarmBoy

The Flynns

Out of the Blue

Mick'sology

Vested Interest

The Importance of Being Ernie with Bonus Book The Importance of

Being Kennedy's

Quirky Girl

<u>For a complete list of Kayt's books, visit:</u>

Kayt's Website: www.kaytmiller.com

ACKNOWLEDGMENTS

Thank you to Olivia at Hot Tree Editing for editing this book
from start to finish.

And an extra special thank you to Becky at Hot Tree
Promotions for your advice, expertise, and your positivity.

And for my beta readers.
Thank you so much for your time and feedback!

ABOUT THE AUTHOR

How did it all start? Well, I love reading and one day I was searching for a book. A book about a certain type of woman and a specific kind of man and I couldn't find it so, I wrote it. I called it Game Changer and it couldn't have been a more appropriate title. It changed my life in many ways. While my real job is teaching young people, my fun job is conjuring up characters and situations to write about.

My goal, as a writer, is to write stories that relate to all of us, to make readers laugh and maybe cry sometimes. I hope my readers can escape into a fantasy, one that's actually possible. Sure, some of the stories could be dubbed "Insta-love" stories but that's okay. I fell in love with my husband pretty damn fast and with my daughter the second I saw her. So, it's a thing, I swear.

Please Follow Me on these social media sites. Following on BookBub to learn about special book deals.

I love hearing from you!

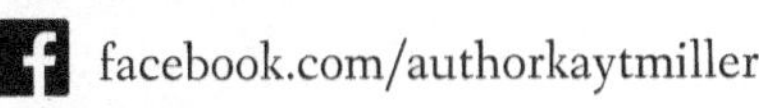 facebook.com/authorkaytmiller

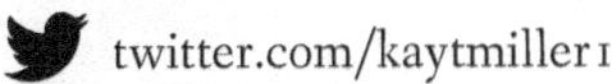 twitter.com/kaytmiller1

 instagram.com/kaytmiller1

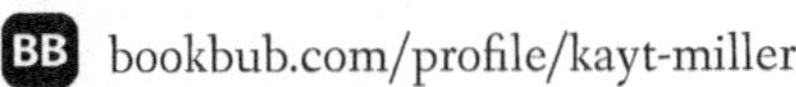 bookbub.com/profile/kayt-miller

COVER DESIGN

The Palmer Sisters Cover Designs
by
Colleen Galligan
galligancolleen@gmail.com

Colleen,
Thank you for all of your hard work
and creativity on the new covers!
I love them! KM

THANK YOU!

Thank you so much for reading Sadie and Charlie's story! When I start a story, it begins with an outline, notes, and lots of crazy thoughts running through my head. When I actually start writing, the characters take over, leading me through the story like they're holding my hand—guiding me. The process is exciting and cathartic. With that said, I hope you enjoy the story.

If you did, please go to my website, www.kaytmiller.com, and join my newsletter so you can be the first to know what's coming up next. And...

And remember...Please, leave a review!

Thank you!

SNEAK PEEK: CORTLAND

A PALMER SISTERS NOVEL 4

Prologue
Cortland

I thought I'd be nervous on my wedding day, but I'm excited as hell. You'd think my family would be all over me about meeting a girl and marrying her two months later, but they haven't been. Not even my mother, who is ordinarily wound tighter than a two-dollar watch, has given me a hard time. No, I think even Emily Ashbury has a lady-crush on my bride-to-be.

Who wouldn't? Polly-Anna Phillips doesn't mince words. She's as real as you can get. It was sure as hell refreshing for me to see, except for the fact that the stubborn woman wouldn't give me a chance. Not for a long-ass time. And damn, I tried to get her attention! She finally agreed, but it was a struggle for nearly a month.

You probably want a little background on all of this before I delve into how I wooed and won the woman of my dreams.

It all started when my big brother, Charles, fell head over heels for Sadie Palmer. It happened in less than a week. I was shocked because Charles Ashbury is a fuddy-duddy, to put it nicely. Don't get me wrong, the man is probably my best friend. I've looked up to him my entire life. He was the perfect big brother. As a kid, I never felt like I was in the way or a burden to him when I wanted to go wherever he was going, which was all the time. So, when he came to me the second night of our Ashbury family cruise aboard the Queen Margaret and told me that he'd found "the one," I wanted to laugh in his face. That was, until I really looked at him. He was serious. Totally no bull-shit, serious.

Not surprisingly, Charles didn't back down, and I watched him work his ass off for five days straight in hot pursuit of one Sadie Palmer, née Rachel Montgomery—her alter-ego on her cruise vacation. Not only that, after Sadie left him in her cabin without a word, he made it his mission to track her down. Two months later, he finally found her out in the boonies of northern Arizona. A mere bakery owner.

Long story short—I know, *too late*—he discovered she was pregnant with *his* kid the day he finally found her again. Now, this is the part that's all Charles Ashbury. Any other man would have heard the words, "I'm pregnant and you're the father," turned on his heel, marched out the door, and hopped on the family jet on his way back to Boston without another thought. But not Charles. He loved Sadie at first sight—a notion I never put much stock in. It's what fairy tales are made of. But I watched the two of them together on the cruise, and then again recently at a family meeting in Page, Arizona, where we learned that my brother is going to be a baby daddy.

I, for one, am thrilled at the idea of having a niece or nephew. The Ashburys have needed something to liven them up for a long time. A little munchkin is just what the doctor ordered. (Ha! Charles is a doctor. Get it?) Seriously, though, my family is boring. The only bright spot in my entire family is my gran, Laura. She's a fucking stitch—always has a smart-ass comment spewing from of her mouth. I adore her.

Now that you've got a little backstory, I can tell you how I met and wooed Polly-Anna Joyce Phillips. Sure, that name is quite a mouthful, but so is my girl. She's delectable. Gorgeous, blonde, curves for days, and a body made for sin. Picture Lana Turner plus Jayne Mansfield merged into one. What? You don't know them? Google them and you'll see. Gran Laura is always watching those old-time movies.

Anyway, the day I walked into Sadie Cakes Bakery and saw her standing there, I knew. My heart started beating so hard at the sight of the blonde bombshell, I thought it was going to burst out of my chest. I stopped breathing for a full minute. Sweat started to gather at my hairline, my palms began to itch, and *I knew*. Hell, she hadn't even seen me yet. When her baby-blues spotted me, she scowled. She fucking scowled. That's when I realized... this girl was more than drop-dead gorgeous. She was special.

Just about every other woman I've ever met has made a move on me. Having the last name Ashbury hasn't hurt, but even women who have no idea who I am fall at my feet. Now, sure, I'm a little vain. Okay, *a lot* vain. If you looked like me, you'd be a little self-centered too. I'm six foot two and fit. I work out nearly every day, usually doing something with a point to it, like kickboxing, biking outside, or my favorite, playing hockey. Along with my rock-hard abs, I've got light brown hair that's styled to perfection, hazel eyes, a wicked smile, and two dimples that drive the ladies crazy.

So, yeah, when Polly gave me that sassy expression and then blew me off, it took me by surprise. Maybe it's the sass that got me interested in the first place. Whatever it was, I decided, then and there, that I would do whatever I could to make her mine, starting with her name. The second I saw the name *Polly* on the name badge pinned to her blue-and-white striped Sadie Cakes Bakery apron, I immediately broke out into song.

"Well, hello, Polly!" Sure, I used the title song of the old movie, *Hello, Dolly!* as my inspiration. So what? It's one of Laura's faves. I've seen it at least ten times. I thought I was clever. It was the perfect icebreaker. But what did the love of my life give me for the effort? An eye roll. That's right. A goddamn eye roll.

'S all right. No problem. I knew I could regroup. I still had game. All I had to do was make a plan. I was good at that. I'm a lawyer, for fuck's sake. I know how to win. And at that moment, I was more determined than ever, muttering to myself, "And win I shall."

Chapter 1

Polly
Two months earlier.

Yeah, I saw him—the hottie that just walked into the bakery. My eyes were drawn to him. Of course they were—he's gorgeous. But the thing is, I've done gorgeous before and it never works out. Not for me, anyway. I'm drawn to those guys like flies to a picnic. Or maybe that's ants to a picnic. Either way, they're my kryptonite. I see them, start to salivate and slobber all over myself, and can barely speak to them.

Now don't get this wrong. I'm *not* a novice or a virgin. Far from it. No, I've been around the block. I've dated plenty of attractive men just like that guy, but I'm done with that. (Okay. Not exactly like that. Confession. Cortland Ashbury is a cut above any guy I've ever seen. The first sight of him made my body feel alive. Charged.) But I'm done with that. Kaput. I'm over the good-looking guys. I need to find myself an old man with a paunch and a bald spot who'll appreciate all that is me.

And there is a lot of me: big ass, big tits, and big thighs. It's how I'm built—just like all the other women in my family. It's my lineage.

Men seem to like that about me, at first. In my experience, men like Cortland are enamored with the idea of the Jayne Mansfield type; Jayne Mansfield with extra padding. The thing is, as soon as they sleep with me once or twice, they're done.

I've accepted my fate. If I end up alone, I'll get myself artificially inseminated when I turn thirty and I'll be fine. No worries.

Turning around to face him, I'm about to ask how I can help him when he opens his mouth. "Well, hello, Polly!" he sings. Yes, that's what I said. He *sang* it, like in that old Barbra Streisand movie.

I'm stunned. I remain silent, thinking that maybe he'd keep going with the song but, sadly, he doesn't. It was sort of funny. No matter, it deserved an eye roll so that's what I gave him before saying, "Hello. Welcome to Sadie Cakes. How can I help you?"

"Marry me. Today."

Great. He's one of those. "No." Short and sweet. Stepping over to the glass cases that house Sadie's treats, I ask, "Would you like some cupcakes?"

He's still smiling at me like a fool. *What is up with this guy?* Maybe he's mentally unstable.

"I'll take a half-dozen assorted cupcakes." He pauses. "And your phone number."

"No." I sigh. "You can have the cupcakes, though."

"Fine. No problem. Cupcakes it is." He winks. "I'll just have to keep trying. Perhaps Sadie will help me out."

"No." She'd better not.

Boxing up six cupcakes, I tell him his total. He hands me a

black American Express card and I roll my eyes again, but he can't see me this time.

Handing him his receipt and a pen, I place the box of his cupcakes into a bag and walk around the counter to hand it to him. "Thank you for shopping at Sadie Cakes."

When he reaches for the bag, our fingers touch, and damn it, a sizzle courses down my arm.

No.

No. No. No.

I won't have it. I won't be attracted to this guy. My heart can't take it. I've already mentally prepared myself for artificial insemination in three or four years. I've accepted it. I'm just not the kind of woman men want to keep. Especially men like this one. It's just the way it is.

I watch him walk out the door in his fancy jeans that were probably made just for him because who can find jeans that fit like that? Rich people, that's who. Couple that with the white tee that was probably $250, but with a couple of holes to make it seem like it was five bucks.

Picking up the pen and his receipt, I stare down at the signature. It's signed Cortland Ashbury in a fairly nice script. Shit. His last name is Ashbury? No doubt he's related to Charlie. A brother? I stare at something else he scribbled down the side of his credit card slip: *Call me, Polly.* 555-332-9801.

Cue eye roll *numéro trois.* I shove the receipt into the drawer.

"No."